The Imaginist

Fairy Tales, Fables, and Folklore

Sharyn G. Jordan

Anthologist

The Imaginist – Fairy Tales, Fables and Folklore
Guiding Grace Series – Volume III
Sharyn G. Jordan, Anthologist

eBook ISBN: 978-1-962570-24-4
Paperback ISBN: 978-1-962570-25-1
Hardcover ISBN: 978-1-962570-27-5
Ingram Spark ISBN: 978-1-962570-26-8
Library of Congress Control Number: 2023921204

Cover Images: Adobe Stock Images
Cover Design: Angie Ayala
Compiler: Sharyn G. Jordan
Interior Design: Marigold2K
Author Photo on Cover: Andrea Harvey Brundage

Publisher: Spotlight Publishing House™
https://spotlightpublishinghouse.com

FengShuiSimplified.com

The Imaginist

Fairy Tales, Fables, and Folklore

Sharyn G. Jordan

Anthologist

SPOTLIGHT
PUBLISHING HOUSE

Goodyear, Arizona

Contents

Dedication

This storybook is dedicated to all who imagine.

Foreword

The enchantment of fairy tales lies not only in their fantastical elements but in the enduring wisdom they impart. They teach us that even in the darkest of times, a glimmer of hope can guide us out of the forest, through the labyrinth and into the light.

These stories have held a place of honor in our culture for centuries. They are the threads that weave the fabric of our collective consciousness, illuminating the human condition, and igniting the fires of creativity.

As you delve into this captivating collection, prepare to be enchanted, enlightened and enlivened. Golden threads of wisdom weave a magic carpet of story, story that blesses the reader with imaginal worlds of wonder--tales that invite us into the deepest parts of ourselves, as women, as mothers, as sisters, as daughters, as lovers of myth and mystery.

The contributors are masters of their craft, wielding words and worlds inspired by ancient folklore, mythology and legend.

No doubt, dear reader, you'll be transported to places where the ordinary and the extraordinary dance in a mesmerizing duet, where fantasy and reality embrace in a passionate tango. In these pages, you will encounter characters whose lives are entwined with magical elements, whether they be ethereal beings, mystical objects, or inexplicable phenomena. You will traverse landscapes where the lines between dreams and wakefulness blur, where boundaries of time and space are but fleeting notions.

This beautiful journey will take you to far-off lands, where wishes come true, where the lessons of old are as relevant today as when whispered around a fire, beneath a starlight sky. Be carried away by the sweeping currents of imaginal worlds, where reality is as fluid as the waters of a mystical river.

Let the words surround you like a warm blanket of blessings, hope, wonder, and love. It is an honor to pen the foreword for this beautiful book. It is a work of art.

Barbara Newman

Greetings from the Imaginist

One of the many, many luminous gifts of an Anthology is the collective energy of pure Joy, the inner alchemizing process of Word Smithing...truly Transformational, and the Power of Story. Celebrating our Writerlies is divine.

With this in mind, it is our great privilege to introduce you to visionary Barbara Newman, author of the award-winning book, The Dreamcatcher Codes. She graces our new section, An Homage to the Storyteller. Her novel is a Love Letter to Mother Earth and her daughters.

Written for the YA genre, yet its noble narrative spans & speaks to all generations. With the Blessings of the sacred GRANDmothers, its timeless tale has REceived EIGHT Prestigous Awards and is making the Hollywood rounds. Indeed, reading her brilliantly cinemascopic novel is an exquisitely enriching inner film experience.

Per Barbara, "Something happens when you listen to your wild soul. It whispers with an urgency, the flame gets fanned, the fire transforms. I didn't know that writing The Dreamcatcher Codes would change me. But it did.

The vision came to me in a lucid dream: four courageous girls coming together from the four directions, powered by earth, air, fire, water, on a search for the stolen Codes of Nature that would restore the natural world. How could I write about Mother Earth if I didn't know her intimately, if I didn't feel her breath in my bones."

~The sentient Barbara visited every sacred site!

Having spent years as a Creative Director, building iconic global brands, upon hearing an interview on NPR about the American Cowgirl, she was so inspired! Barbara is an advocate for building cultural bridges and empowering women and girls and was part of the think tank that developed the Fred Rogers Center for Children's Media and Education. She lives in the Berkshire Mountains of Western, MA, on Stockbridge-Munsee Mohican land.

~Deep Bow.

Sharyn G. Jordan-McWhorter

Prologue

"As sacred Storytellers,
we are Alchemists, Apothecaries,
and Architects of a Pristine Future.
We are the Muse, the Mythmaker, and the Magician."
—Sharyn G. Jordan-McWhorter

*P*lease brew a sweet CUPPA, cozy into your favorite nook, and pour yourself into our exquisite anthology, *The Imaginists, A Storybook of Fairy Tales, Fables, and Folklore*. You will meet illustrious people who bend, mend, and wend time and space. They live in charmed places, such as an enchanted forest where Tree Spirits whisper, Owls speak, and Ancestors murmur to our hearts. Not too far away is a divine Dream Weaver who dwells in a coral castle by the sea. In a nearby mansion are majestic mirrors that elongate our perception, enhance our ingenuity, and elevate our every thought.

In a world where anything and everything is possible, think of the blessings of having your very own Avatar. Or, as in our promiscuous (unrestricted) preponderance, is the Protagonist's proposal of BEing an *Ava-STARR*. Boldly, they do one's bidding; BEstow wonder and awe and BEhave bravely through their BEqueathed Superpowers. Where did these heroic *Ava-STARRS* REceive their galactic prowess? From their Creators, our brilliant Authors, of course. In such vivid imagination, our exceptional *Ava-STARR*s are encoded with Refined, REspectful, and REsourceful Real-Life Wisdom Gained.

These BEmusing chronicles will readily REcall your sweet days of youth, which developed your inventiveness, stretched you BEyond Limitations, and enthused you to push back your horizons. These enduring, endearing, and enriching narratives of the heart arched you into an ever-expanding kingdom where joy, beauty, and dreams REside.

Consider and experience, albeit embrace, these magnificently magical Ava-STARRS. Since we are the stories we tell ourselves, this elegant Anthology's intention is to align you with your innate creativity, activate your inner child's curiosity, and cultivate the inherent Storyteller REsiding in your Soul.

You will appreciate, RElate, and REsonate with the realities of our Ava-STARR's inimitable challenges, truths, and specific era. *The Imaginists Storybook* is a cohesive collection that takes you on a journey through mysterious, mystical, and mythical realms. Each chapter weaves ancient archetypes, the power of symbolism, and/or a flair for adventure into the plot.

Historically, these imminently iconic tales provide exceptional insights into BEing Conflict REsolutionts, Overcomers, and Catalysts of Positive Change. Oh, how True Love's REdemptive value will move you! Our REgal illustrations will enthrall you with the stunningly spectacular quests of the admirable *Ava-STARRS,* and you will BE Inspired to untether your luminous imagination. Indeed, writing takes courage, yet you, our dearest Reader, have what it takes to pen your dreams into BEing.

In addition to singing the praises of our superb Fairytellers, Fablists, and Folklorists, we are honored to REmember those tender Souls who have gone on their Ethereal Journey BEfore us. The Legacy section titled "In Memory Of..." is an homage to their ongoing gifts of wisdom, wit, and warmth.

Gently, whether they turned their pain into purpose and/or passion into posterity, we celebrate and cherish their lives. We have been REminded of just how precious yet temporary our Earthly Sojourning is. Let Us BE Whom We Love as a tribute to them and in the abundant spirit of creating a kind, illuminating, and compassionate life.

Our World Builder Episode brings attention to Difference-Makers. These intrepid visionaries, bloggers, JOY-Bringers, and podcasters generously pave a pathway of uplifting positivity, intrinsic possibilities, and great, good potentialities, provoking us to BE our Best Selves.

Always REmember,

"We are sacred Storytellers, the Alchemist, the Apothecary, and the Architect of our Pristine Future.
We are the Muse, the Mythmaker, and the Magician."

Writerly yours,

Sharyn G. Jordan-McWhorter

Anthologist, Storyteller & Home Whisperer
FengShuiSimplified.com ~Founded in 1994

Fairy Tales,
Fables and Folklore

Ode to the Imaginist

Oh, Imaginists, our experiential writing
'Tis a MORAL to Fable's Myth, so exciting
Net-weaving with our luminous PEN Warriors
Keen Visionaries, BOLD, & courageous Storiers.

Nurtured from WISDOM Keepers
Ephemeral expressions, sublime Speakers
Imagination, an inner landscape's SYNERGY
Of the enchanted woods and oceans' ENERGY.

JOY, a catalyst, cascades beyond infinity
Mindset, attitude, and BE•liefs of Positivity
BEing inspired cultivates salubrious sanguinity
Optimism seeds blessings & breeds synchronicity.

BE an Overcomer, a BRAVE, bold BEcomer
BE a SAGE, a Shaman, an indigenous Drummer
We EMBRACE the challenge, double down, and Dare.
As Obstacle RE•movers, brilliant EDUCATORs of Care

We are Life's narrator, its author & SCRIBE
In our Dream Circle, heavenly HeART's our Tribe
BEing Bright, luminous, a sublime SPIRITUAL essence
BEing Fluid & FLOWING; centered in Divinity's Presence.

Evolving ancient archetypal patterns' allegories
Downloading, Wordsmithing GRATITUDE stories

CASTing mindful, sagacious characters most wise
Let us channel the eternal BOUNTY of open blue skies.

CREATE an enriching dialogue, discoverable
From the Soul, wonder-filled, in AWE, so vulnerable.
Pleaza install Environmental HEALING's illuminations
As nature itself ELEVATES sumptuous Self-RE•velations.

Of beauty & bliss, we elegantly enthuse
Brewing a divine CUPPA, inviting our MUSE
Sacred STORYTELLing Sagas, Legends, Lore
We EDIFY, Script, Cowork, Conspire, and ADORE.

Oh, such timeless tales FULLY RE•plete
With our WORDS, we delight, unite & are complete
Focus on BEing charitable, of generous affirmations
OUR passionate intentions, aspirations, & inclinations.

OUR thoughts, syllables, deeds foretell
Unfold in the very WORLD where we dwell
If we do not agree with our LEGACY's History
Instead, PEN a novel of worth, solve the mystery.

Edit, delete, change, REFINE the prose
CLAIM our inner Treasure, a BEjeweled RE•pose
With each beat, RE•sonate, RE•connect & RENEW
Syncopate, Sing, SHINE, Dance, and Breakthrough.

Deep bow to our fellow Imaginists of GIVING
Together, we traverse this Tao of Exquisite Living
Of ethnicity, culture, creed's tired polarity, RISE ABOVE
To BE Loved Unequivocally & to Unconditionally BE LOVE.

~Sharyn G. Jordan-McWhorter, © 2013, 2023

Chapter 1

Alicia Bravo

Alicia Bravo is a native of four generations living in the Arizona desert. She is a passionate, intuitive hair salon owner and colorist/artist/stylist. Since the beginning of her career, her first love has been writing. This led to life experiences such as confessions and juicy secrets heard from behind her salon chair. This driving force led to the chapter in this book about the magic mirror. Seeing people when they gaze into the mirror made Alicia realize that people don't always see themselves as they really are.

This inspired her to write about how we are quick to judge ourselves. Sometimes it takes life experiences and wounds to help us see how we may have grown into who we have become. How we handle the truth is a conscious choice we make every single day. To gaze into a mirror — really into ourselves — we can truly embrace who we have become, or make a change if we don't like what we see. Being able to see people for who they truly are and listen closely to their stories represents Alicia's greatest gifts.

Contact information:

602-579-9046
https://www.instagram.com/bravosalonaz/
https://www.facebook.com/BravoSalonAZ
https://bravosalonaz.com/the-owner/
https://www.linkedin.com/in/alicia-bravo-18942511/

For Our Video Interview with Alicia Bravo scan the QR Code with your smartphone, or view via this link:
https://youtu.be/6lv0KfYWNuk

Amyrrah
and the Magic Mirror

By Alicia Bravo

"A man or woman who tells the truth
doesn't mind being questioned. A liar does."
~ Alicia Bravo

Amyrrah
and the Magic Mirror

You're More Than You Think You Are

By Alicia Bravo

There once lived a girl named Amyrrah. She lived far away in a high mountain palace. Amyrrah was born a princess and was happy and quite fortunate. Her parents, King Salman and Queen Salana, were very proud of Amyrrah because she was quite beautiful. As a young girl at age 12, she was a child prodigy in the arts and music. Her parents often took Amyrrah to their elegant private parties and had her play the piano and display her paintings. Amyrrah was a hit among everyone, and they loved her performances and artwork.

One evening, the king and queen prepared to attend a dance very far away and decided not to take Amyrrah with them. They left her at the palace with her nanny because they would be gone for several days. On the way back from the weekend of celebrating, the king and queen were in a terrible accident. The king was injured, and the queen perished. Amyrrah was devastated. While healing from his accident, the king was inconsolable at losing his queen. He became reclusive and distant from Amyrrah in his grief. Amyrrah blamed her father for her mother's death and never forgave him.

Amyrrah grew up quickly and became more beautiful. However, she despised her father and internalized her grief over her mother's death. She held all her feelings inside, became overweight, and hated the way she had become. Amyrrah felt like part of herself had perished with her mother and she became depressed.

The palace wizard was a well-educated wise man, healer, and astronomer named Talizman. Talizman had watched the princess for some time and noticed all the changes occurring in her life. Talizman needed help in his laboratory and scriptorium, so he decided to ask Amyrrah to become his assistant. He wanted to teach her all about the stars and potions, tinctures and syrups that heal people. Talizman knew Amyrrah was truly made for this kind of work and thought this would be a way to help the princess heal her own grief.

Something happened in the scriptorium to Amyrrah that stopped her in her tracks. Amyrrah stumbled upon Talizman's magic mirror. Amyrrah had never seen herself before as she had in this mirror. Amyrrah couldn't believe her eyes. When she saw herself, she began to cry. She saw her own beauty but couldn't look upon herself long because of what she had become. "This magic mirror is the Mirror of Truth," said Talizman. "What you see is your TRUE SELF. Look deeper into the mirror, Amyrrah," said Talizman.

Amyrrah couldn't bear to see herself and began to weep uncontrollably. Talizman said, "This is no ordinary mirror, Amyrrah. You must accept what you have become; however, there is always a way to change if you are willing." Amyrrah despised mirrors. She told Talizman to cover the mirror at once, and then ordered her father to banish all mirrors throughout their kingdom.

King Salman wanted his daughter's forgiveness and affection, so he immediately gave the order to banish all mirrors across the land. All mirrors were to be broken and burned so that no one could look upon themselves. Talizman, knowing that his mirror was enchanted and therefore could never be banished, took the mirror and hid it deep in the palace dungeon where no one ever went except for him. He covered it with an enchanted cloak of protection made from a golden goat's skin which rendered it invisible. The enchanted mirror could only reveal itself when the time was right and only a charmed person could make it be seen again. Talizman had invoked a spell on the magic mirror to reveal itself only to the one who could see themselves in the true light.

As the years passed, Amyrrah grew more beautiful and stronger. She became skilled in Talizman's work in astronomy, tinctures, potions, and became more attuned to the universe. She was growing wise, and skilled in wizardry and was now a healer in her own right.

Amyrrah was so hungry for knowledge and buried herself in work that she wasn't as hungry for food. She connected to Talizman's work in such a deep way that she didn't stop learning and was becoming a seer. Talizman often sent her into the woods to gather herbs, plants, special water, and minerals for his potions and tinctures.

Talizman gave Amyrrah a special tea every day, healing her body, helping her become more alert and slimmer. Without knowing it, Amyrrah was healing both inside and out. She was feeling lighter at a soul level, gaining invaluable knowledge through Talizman's guidance.

One day, Talizman sent Amyrrah down to the dungeon to fetch a special glass bottle for a tincture he was concocting. Amyrrah had never been down there before, and Talizman knew it was time for her to learn more. Amyrrah couldn't find the special glass bottle. She lit the torch brighter and saw a faint glow at the other end of the dungeon. She wasn't afraid, but curious. As she got closer, the glow became brighter and brighter. As she approached the glowing object, it called out her name. The object was shrouded in mystery. She removed the cloak and the mirror revealed itself to her. The mirror lit up and Amyrrah saw herself. She couldn't believe her reflection in the mirror. She touched her face and then the mirror. The minute she touched the mirror, her hand went through it. She then went into the mirror, came out on the other side and saw her mother waiting there.

The place was ethereal, covered in clouds, and she heard mystical music. Amyrrah had been transported into another dimension. Her mother was ready to embrace her and Amyrrah was so delighted. She spent an entire day with her mother. The queen took her daughter all over and showed her what had happened to the kingdom after Amyrrah had all the mirrors removed.

What had happened to her father, the king? He was a shell of himself, a miser, drunk, unfit to rule and her mother said that Amyrrah needed to make amends with her father to help him heal, which would also heal the kingdom. The people had become uncaring, unable to see themselves and were blinded by their own mistrust. They became empty and lost.

Amyrrah asked her mother if she could visit again. Her mother said, "Of course, but you must first heal the land and kingdom. Make all the mirrors visible again so people can see themselves once more. Make amends with your father and the people. Then come back to me through the magic mirror. I will await your return."

When Amyrrah came back through the mirror to the current dimension, she saw her own reflection and couldn't believe how beautiful she had become. She loved herself! She felt elated with a joy that she hadn't experienced since before her mother died. She knew then her destiny in life and what her life purpose was. Amyrrah wanted to become a great leader and realized that it was time for her to make a difference in her kingdom and all the land.

Amyrrah then loved the mirror and thanked the Mirror of Truth for showing her who she had truly become. Without this journey and all its wounds, she couldn't have become the person she now was. Amyrrah went to Talizman and said that she never found the special bottle, but she found the magic mirror instead. Talizman said, "It was the right time for you to discover the mirror. Only you could see it, for it was invisible. Only one who could see the truth would be able to invoke the mirror."

Amyrrah knew it was time for her to take responsibility and make amends with the people, especially with her father, so they could all be whole again.

Amyrrah thanked Talizman for saving the magic mirror and helping her heal from her own grief. Talizman said, "I needed another person in this land with wisdom and knowledge." He knew it was Amyrrah because the mirror had told him to seek her out to help her become more aware and stronger in the truth of her being.

Amyrrah then became a wise sage and gentle ruler alongside her father, King Salman. She also had the guidance of the seer, Talizman. The mirror was displayed in a place that became the center of the palace, where it was regarded as the most sacred room. Amyrrah had become a great healer helping people see themselves as they TRULY are.

Chapter 2

Becky Norwood

#1 International Bestselling author, speaker, & book publishing expert, **Becky Norwood** is CEO of *Spotlight Publishing House*™. She is widely recognized for the empowering and intuitive way she guides others to weave storytelling into their books and marketing. She incorporates her methods with sound marketing that is the pathway for business expansion and audience growth.

Becky has brought over 400 authors to #1 bestseller through her publishing house. Countless listeners have heard her interviews of both authors and experts offering sage advice. She offers an extensive catalog of services supporting emerging and established authors.

Becky believes that a well-told story is a gateway for growth, sharing, and a way to unite humanity. She is an advocate for the positive that comes from sharing our creative genius and impacting our world in positive ways.

She and her husband Mark reside in Goodyear, Arizona with their two darling canine pets, Jesse aka Peekers, and Molly aka Polly Wolly Doodle All Day, and Miss Molly Magoo a Puddy. They have a combined family of five adult kids and 12 grandchildren.

Website: https://spotlightpublishinghouse.com
Email: becky@spotlightpublishinghouse.com

Facebook: https://www.facebook.com/SpotlightBookPublishing
LinkedIn: https://www.linkedin.com/in/beckybnorwood/
Instagram: https://www.instagram.com/spotilghtpublishinghouse/

Fable of

Honey Bee Happy

Adapted for Becky BEE Norwood
by Sharyn G. Jordan

"One must have chaos to give birth to a dancing star."
~Friedrich Nietzsche

The Fable of

Honey Bee Happy

Adapted for Becky BEE Norwood
by Sharyn G. Jordan

On the magical night of the mystical Harvest Moon, I was born to my majestic mother, Arianna Rose. Descending from the Celestial Realms of the Golden Orb into the depths of Mother Earth, I was the answer to her lifetime of prayers of birthing a daughter. At 33 years of age, Mother was the youngest Medicine Woman ever to serve at the Temple of Divine Love. Our ancestors gifted Mother the ability to speak with the sacred mountains, hear the whispers of the enchanted woods, and understand mythical archetypal totems of the forest animals. Her sing-song language was so ethereal it sounded like French, Spanish, and Romanian had majestically merged. She is also the sublime sister of my Aunt Luna from the Silver Moon and the beautiful BEE, Queen of her BeeHive Tribe.

I chose my magnificent mother and her siblings from 8,000 lifetimes of having lived in over 2,000 magnificent galaxies. At least 3,500 of my incarnations found me guiding souls from the living realities to Glory. For eons, I have been also known as the River of Time, answering the Current's calling. I flow, weave, and meander in the silver-lined pockets of wisdom. By choosing wisely lifetime after lifetime has found me uplifting humanity, creating divine portals of beauty and bliss and especially joy. Since I have mastered the exquisite energy of being happy, I have come in to assist my mother and her sisters' commitment to elevating the precious peoples of Earth. To teach that they are beloved children of a benevolent Universe. Now, in its last shift of the ages, Earth finds itself in old patterns of destruction, chaos, and war. Yet, with gratitude, love, and, yes, happiness, just as its habitants, she is also destined to become a luminous Star.

Through patterns of chaos, mankind has forgotten its birthright of being divine. Instead, many experience the despair of loss, grief, and sorrow. The planet's inhabitants have been hijacked by fear, plagued by shame, and disconnection from Mother Nature. Humanity's well-being is at risk. Having descended to Earth in this era, I committed to witness and overcome these struggles firsthand. Yes, happiness, as in joy, is an inside job; it is from this very essence that renewal is always possible. Once true happiness is absorbed into the souls of those who seek it, true transformation occurs. From the wisdom of ages, humanity has been blessed with the power of connection that exists between nature, the divine, and humans. Leaning into gratitude, choosing to love unconditionally, and dwelling in happiness, humanity and the earth's vibration are elevated.

To help download this profound process, every month on the night of the full moon, Mother Arianna Rose gathered together with my aunt. This particular time was most appropriate as it was the Harvest Moon. Dedicated to not only welcoming me into this world but also to bless me with my highly energetic, meaningful name. As we know, our earthly moniker's encoding provides part of the essential support required to fulfill our Destiny. Mother looked to the heavens for signs, symbols, and answers; she was dancing around and embracing my infant self while singing her harmonious supplications. When the three sisters lifted me to the skies, Mother's attention was drawn to the magical Milky Way. She was in awe to witness an enriching golden honey pouring out into the night skies. Its elixir glazed billions of stars, creating an otherworldly luster's luminous glow. Thus, my name, HONEY, was ever so divinely inspired.

Long ago, Mother predetermined I would be named to honor her sister Bee. Now, she is not your Mayberry's apple-pie-baking Aunt Bee. Her luxuriously thick, black hair is, of course, pulled up in an elegant, forever classic chignon, bee•hive style, crowned by a stunning black diamond tiara. Wearing onyx-hued leggings and satin tunic, she flaunts her custom-made, striped black and golden velvet robe. She is a sublime sight to behold. With her luminescent wings, this queen is the very essence of a mythical creature with powerful magic. She is revered, respected, and redeemed. The productivity of a life well lived is not only purpose-filled, but it is passionately experiential. Therefore, I was HONEY BEE.

My Aunt Luna was stunning in her silvery gossamer gown and shimmering pewter-colored cloak, which accentuated her glowing white hair. Her brilliant golden crown of stars and mini-moons was a gift from Jupiter himself. As her statuesque body stands regal and actually glistens against the backdrop of her full moon, her Aunt Luna is stunning in her silvery gossamer gown. Draped over her shoulders was a pewter-colored cloak accentuating her glowing white hair, which was crowned by a diamond-studded tiara. Her shimmering, statuesque body stands regal and actually glistens against the backdrop of her full moon. Known as the Goddess of the Divine Feminine, her pearl-orbed staff commands the entire night sky. Also, within her mastery is a place for Awakened Dreamers. Throughout all the ages, Aunt Luna enabled people to better connect with their spiritual potential. She represents intuition, nurturing our relationships, and the changes life is forever presenting, as in the ebb and flow of the tides. She is also associated with the inner journey of the mystic. This is where happiness looms large.

Ah, now named Honey Bee Happy and true to my preconceived notions of this lifetime, I would learn to trust this name. Privy to sorrow, grief, and human tragedy by way of my childhood friends who entrusted me with their secrets of suffering and sadness, I held sacred, circled space for them. For these male and female friends of all ages, I was a bridge over their troubled waters. Within this safe environment, they were tenderly respected, embraced, and loved. In their own time, they released traumatic troubles, allowing healing tears to pour forth. Indeed, renewal was present.

With our sacred circle's positive ripple effects, my mother, Arianna Rose, my aunts Luna, Bee, and I were granted unlimited access to the Temple of Divine Love. Furthering the Sacred Circles of Healing opportunities, our ancient yet timeless teachings focused on soul growth, higher consciousness, and transcendence. People from all over the world flocked to our classes learning how to go into their inner realms beyond the ordinary where meaning, magic, and miracles dwell. This wisdom connected our students with something much greater than themselves. Through mindfulness, meditation, and their inner muse, these enriching experiences ushered in a sense of unity, peace, and transformation. Available to each of them and to all of humanity are the blessings of connectivity, empathy, and the power of uplifting one another.

In your own sacred circle, as a beloved child of the benevolent universe, let us BEE One with Nature, the Divine, and edify our fellow Humanity. And, Honey, BEE Happy!

Chapter 3

Chelsea Sutton

Chelsea Sutton is a nationally known equine sports announcer and founded The ConsultMent Agency, a marketing firm that provides marketing consulting and management for brands in hospitality, professional services and horse events.

From startups to multi-million-dollar companies, The ConsultMent Agency has managed accounts with 150k followers, gained millions of impressions per year, and impacted revenue growth of over 20% increase year over year.

Her love for business & problem solving brings a strategic business-driven approach to marketing. While Chelsea writes thousands of words each week in marketing material, her contribution to The Imaginist is her first fiction piece.

Chelsea graduated top of her class in Entrepreneurship and Business Management from Arizona State in 2012. Originally from Buffalo NY, she grew up on a horse farm in North Carolina, and now resides in Arizona. When not at her desk or behind a microphone, you can find her swing dancing, riding her horse.

Chelsea runs ConsultMent with her high-school sweetheart of 16+ years, Travis, and they are now expecting their first child.

CONTACT INFORMATION
Chelsea Sutton
Cell: 252-717-991
Email: Chelsea@ConsultMent.Agency

Website: ConsultMent.Agency

Social:
Facebook: https://www.facebook.com/chelseasuttonofficial
Instagram: https://www.instagram.com/chelseasuttonofficial
LinkedIn: https://www.linkedin.com/in/chelseajdsutton

Scan the QR Code with your smartphone or go to https://youtu.be/PWXW-_QsPr4 to watch our video interview with Chelsea.

The Vine Blinds
In The Family Room

"Every day you have a choice.
Dress for chance, or dress for your choice."

The Vine Blinds
In The Family Room

By Chelsea Sutton

*R*ippling sounds of cracks and crunching roared as the vines ripped, the openings were exposed, and the warmth of the tree house wafted away like a whisper in the wind.

After toiling for hours, trying to find strength in her wings to pick up the strained branches, Harmony gave up. She was physically exhausted and emotionally depleted. There were no more tears left to cry. No attempt to reposition the greens would create the fortress that once stood.

Harmony was devastated. Everything she worked for was gone. What hurt the most was Rupert's betrayal. How could he do this? He knew about all the years of work. He saw the hours of time she spent, planting, nurturing, harvesting. He had to have known what those vines meant to her, right? He had been a part of the community from the beginning.

The tree house wasn't just a play pen. This was a sacred sanctuary for sustainability and for sanity. A safe place for frivolous play and friendships to be forged. The ground level was Harmony's home: a kitchen, small bedroom and her intention closet. Each morning begins with prayer journaling, then outfit sourcing. Harmony scoured the closet to find the elements essential to translate her intentions. Black and white clothes meant a decisive attitude. Sandals were a sign she was up for short adventures and fast flight — she loved the wind on her toes.

The second level was "The Family Room." That's what Harmony called it. It was open to anyone from the community, as long as they had been invited by someone else, agreed on the house rules, helped when help was needed, and on occasion brought food enough to share. Everything happened in The Family Room. Kids brought their coloring books. Different species interacted like family. Even negotiations — last year, Charlie traded her magical paint brushes for Katarina's magical bagpipes — and magical trades rarely happen.

Magic works differently in each layer of the forest. Here, the forest folk look human with animal-like features and a magical power. Sometimes those are one in the same: Harmony's hummingbird wings allow her to fly with lightning speed and lift unexplainable weights. Katarina has a horse mane, long like Rapunzel, but her magic is her bagpipe. When a stranger blows, it sounds like a broken instrument, but when Katarina plays, the sound is so pure that it stills anyone within audible distance.

Harmony spent much of her time with forest folk, coincidentally becoming a mentor to them, talking them through challenging circumstances and being a wise ear to hear when they had lost their way. Harmony knew the forest needed a physical space to facilitate this. Harmony didn't want to choose between being home and being with the friends she cared for. The family room was where her community and her sanctuary could collide.

Building the second story wasn't just nails and boards, walls and doors: nature needed to be integrated. For those who live in the forest to be comfortable in some of their most uncomfortable experiences, what better a room than one where the lines between forest and family room blurred. The walls are recycled wood from fallen trees held together by pig putty, the furniture is animal hide from the forest floor gathered by the folk. The vine blinds were the most laborious work.

The windows had bothered Harmony for some time. The space felt empty with uncovered windows. A draft would come in, steal the secrets, and usher them into the woods for the entire forest to hear.

The day Harmony discovered the vines was a day she'll never forget. Flowing with nature, she sported a whimsical brown dress tied at the waist with a well-worn piece of leather. She accompanied the dress with turquoise, the type of necklace that you notice before anything else. Turquoise was one of her favorite stones. Varying in color from green to blue, with veins and specks, much like Harmony herself. An array of colors, a combination of patterns, just as her name signifies; not a balance, but a blend; not perfect, but pretty; nothing is identical, everything is intentional.

Scouring the forest, there it was: Grandmother Weeping Eucalyptus. Harmony's mother loved the weeping willow. As a child, Harmony would sit under the willow tree after a tough day. The thick trunk felt safe, even when the changing winds moved the branches. For generations, forest folk used Eucalyptus to soothe the throat, heal a chest cold, release tense muscles in a hot springs bath, and girls would rub it on their neck if they thought their date might be "the one."

For weeks, she begged Grandmother Weeping Eucalyptus for her blessings to use the branches for The Family Room. After countless morning talks, extra snacks of sunshine, gifts of fresh water from the river, what finally convinced Grandma W.E. was a visit from the regulars. The Family Room folk sat with Grandma, telling stories of the friendships flourishing, the romance rekindled, the magical powers magnified. On the big visit, Harmony wore that same turquoise necklace she wore the day she discovered the tree. As the forest folk told their stories, Harmony held that necklace, rubbing her thumb over the last triangular stone, as it dangled down her bosom. It was as if she found contentment, as if Harmony said "I trust you" with her touch.

That marked the 20-year journey in growing the blinds of The Family Room. She planted and watered that first tree, checking on it daily. She planted the second, and third, to ensure the first wasn't lonely. The blinds needed to be thick enough to hold warmth in and friendship together through even the toughest times. Hours she toiled trimming and guiding the limbs. Harmony created anchors from deer antlers. Three harsh winters almost killed the trees, but Harmony made sure to clothe them at night, provide extra shade during the sleet, and stayed up late to read them tales.

The windows grew a lush woven covering from the weeping floral Eucalyptus. All the folk loved them for one reason or another. Rule No. 10 was "No hanging, climbing or pulling on the vines." It was among other House Rules such as Rule No. 3 "No stealing others' magical tools" and Rule No. 5 "When offense is made, so must an apology." The rules were designed to protect the culture of the community. Harmony added rule 10 after the vines had grown thick, as a way to protect the past.

After 7,395 days the vines came crashing down. Rupert decided to use the vines to get into The Family Room, instead of the stairs. After a heavy rain the vines couldn't hold his weight. All of the vines were alive and intertwined; thus, all the windows lost their coverings, the Weeping Eucalyptus lost its branches, and The Family Room lost its protection.

Forest fairies like Harmony are stringent rule-followers, but Harmony had a weak spot. Harmony didn't want to hurt those she loved. While altruistic, that was her downfall. She made excuses for Rupert. Maybe he was in a hurry or had trouble at work. What kept her up at night was the consequence of Rule No 10: suspension from the treehouse. Rupert would have to find a new community. Harmony couldn't bear the thought. It was miles and miles before the next tree community, and many of them weren't welcoming to new members.

What if Rupert got frostbite on his way? Or worse, what if another community wasn't as gracious as they were, as the suspension for another vine crash was death?

Everything Harmony stood for boiled down to love. Harmony felt the suspension would send a message that she didn't love Rupert, and it made her sick to her stomach.

For days her wings wouldn't work. Walking around the garden, she would use wagons and baskets to transport slowly what her wings once would once wisp away in an instant. Her bright pastel spots turned into gloomy grays. While she pretended she was ok, other forest animals could tell she wasn't herself.

As the days passed, something strange began to happen. The energy shifted. Other tree animals started to grumble. Each day fewer came to the tree house, and they stopped bringing enough food to share. What was once a bustling commonplace was now desolate.

For days, Harmony avoided Rupert. It felt selfish to punish him. "I can rebuild," she told herself. She worried suspension would hurt him. What if he never came back. Then, she began to realize it was bigger than her. Harmony noticed that Rule No. 10 wasn't just about protecting what she had built for herself, it was about protecting the environment for the Forest Folk. It was about upholding and protecting the building that protected the others.

Harmony knew what she had to do, and she knew she had to do it quickly, before the furry folk lost all connection to The Family

Room, and worse, to each other. She put on a soft cotton black dress, work boots, hair in a bun, her strong turquoise necklace, and headed to find Rupert.

Chapter 4

Cynthia Young

Cynthia Young, CEFSP, CTSS, is a Certified Essential Feng Shui Practitioner and Trauma Support Specialist living near Phoenix, Arizona. She works with groups, individuals and trauma survivors to help them better understand how to support their authenticity and understand how painful past experiences can affect how we live and thrive in our spaces.

Cynthia is a graduate of the Western School of Feng Shui. She has also earned certificates in Non-Violent Communication practitioner training and functional medicine and complex trauma support. She specializes in residential and commercial Feng Shui, landscape energy design, and co-creating trauma-informed spaces.

Drawing on her experience as a medical trauma survivor, experiencing a hemiplegic stroke on the first day of first grade, she opened her business, Asteya Studios, LLC, which is an integration of trauma-informed support and Feng Shui guidance. She has spoken to groups at the International Feng Shui Guild and the London School of Feng Shui, among others. She studied and practiced near Boston for many years before moving to the Southwest.

For more details, please visit:
www.asteyastudios.com

Instagram: https://www.instagram.com/asteyastudios_feng_shui/
Facebook: asteyastudios-Feng Shui and Meditation
LinkedIn: https://www.linkedin.com/in/cynthia-young-9663076b/

To watch our video interview with Cynthia, scan the QR Code with your smartphone or go to:
https://youtu.be/Cv5f6m4yu5U

Nourishing Fae Sing Glory

How the Feng Carried Me
By Cynthia Young

"Santosha invites us into contentment by taking refuge in a calm center, opening our hearts in gratitude for what we do have, and practicing the paradox of 'not seeking.'"

Deborah Adele, quote from her book entitled,
"The Yamas & Niyamas:
Exploring Yoga's Ethical Practice"
(2009)

Nourishing Fae Sing Glory

By Cynthia Young

could see the outline of his beak in the water. My wings were still moist from the overnight dew where I slept. I raced past a lotus that stood upright in the morning breeze. Circling back, I touched down on its pink blossoms, trying to catch my breath. I was fighting for my life! I had escaped the starken many times before, having been fast enough to evade its razor-sharp talons and pointed beak. They were a natural enemy to all the winged creatures of Greshen Pond.

Greshen Pond had always been my home with glistening waters and tall grasses that offered a lush place to sleep and dry off as the Feng blew lightly. The reeds were the last line of safety because directly beyond them was the entrance to the darkness of the Denzund Forest. It was home to the starken, the dangerous birds that fed upon dragonflies, mice and honeybees. My four-winged body kept me dancing within the pond's edges where I felt safe.

I perched on the lotus, nibbling on a petal. I gazed down and saw my reflection. Controlling each of my wings, I maneuvered to a silent hover over the green lily pad. Suddenly an ominous sound rang past me! The gush was so fierce that it made me tumble into the water. The starken's sharp claws grasped at me as I fumbled. His body was too heavy to hover over me, so he flew upward, readying for another attack. He dove straight down, beak wide open. He struck me and I tumbled into the water again, submerged beneath the surface. Everything became slow motion. I couldn't move and felt the underwater grasses pushing me along the current.

The reeds carried me to a small spot at the edge of the pond. I could hear the lapping of water as my wings soaked up the sun. I stumbled, but managed a slight hover as my feet perched on small pebbles. Gazing upward, I froze. Just beyond was the entrance to Denzund Forest, its wide-mouthed darkness glaring menacingly.

I was still clearing water from my wings when I heard it again. The swoosh of feathers, the curdling scream. This time the starken hit me, hard! I tumbled and spun as a small piece of my wing ripped. I scrambled to fly, fluttering as fast as I could. I heard the scream again, so I ducked behind a tree at the entrance to the forest. Clinging to a quivering leaf, I sat motionless. The starken abandoned his attack as he became preoccupied with a rabbit. My wing was slightly damaged, which would slow my flight speed. There was no turning back to Greshen Pond. The only way to survive was through the fearful forest. I recoiled at the thought.

Earth

I entered the forest, breathless from being attacked. A familiar buzz was welcomed as I devoured a group of mosquitoes just beyond the dewy shrubs. I fluttered my recovering wings and became enraptured by the sand-colored earth. There were speckles of brightly shining mineral deposits along the bank. Landing there, I felt the breeze engulf me and sleep overtake me. Everything was still. I felt connected and safe in my shining grotto. I was grounded.

Metal

Upon awakening, I caught a glimpse of a small black insect dancing on a green leaf. It proved a perfect breakfast. My wings felt more aligned and the slight tear on my hindwing didn't seem to cause a problem. Slowly, I glided through the area, enjoying the dew illuminated by the morning sun. The Feng whisked me through the crisp air with ease, but then increased in intensity. I rushed through a grove of tall trees and gasped slightly as they cleared. Before me was a sparkling cove of rocks. I swooped down to investigate and landed on a small quartz perched atop a pile of beautiful crystals. I sat for awhile, wondering if it would be safe to turn back and rejoin my life at Greshen Pond. My pondering was interrupted by the familiar croak of a forest frog. Not wanting another battle, I flew up and out of the grotto.

Water

A small stream cut through the forest as the sun hid behind some clouds. I followed the stream's path, meandering through the richly colored leaves and making a quick pivot at a fallen tree. My wings caught the steady Feng that was driving me towards a destination. I was processing the chase of the starken and letting the water's path refresh my determination to make it through the Denzund Forest alive.

Wood

There was a rustle of leaves, a shrieking squeak and an explosion of fur. I darted into a hollow tree. Wings tucked back, I sat silent. Then I saw him. He had tufted ears, small black eyes, sharp but paired teeth, followed by a bushy tail. He sniffed, scratched and stuffed small acorns into his cheeks. He humorously toddled through the forest in search of food. I decided that I too wanted food as the water I tracked hadn't yielded any nourishment.

I followed him. He bobbled and ran with a flit, occasionally stopping to raise his eyes to look for threats and more acorns. He squealed and ran so quickly that his full cheeks made him tumble into a somersault. I watched him, then looked at the tall trees and filtered sunlight dancing across the lush green growth. My decision not to go back to Greshen Pond was feeling stronger. The unknown was in front of me, and I felt the trees beckon me deeper into their canopy. The growing whisper of something new was echoing against this backdrop.

The roar was loud and startled me. A looming screech and growl were in the nearby field. I couldn't see my awkward friend, but I heard him scurry across to safety under a patch of moss, abandoning acorns along the way. Crash! I could see one of the trees fall, striking the hard ground with a BANG! A silent veil fell over the forest. I stayed on my log, frozen and terrified. I heard the squirrel again, which prompted me to move. I flew. Now I could only hear a slight growling in the distance.

Fire

The darkness of the forest was serene. I flew quietly between clumps of leaves and fallen bark. Chasing some unsuspecting black flies made for a delicious dinner. It seemed unusually warm. As I flew through the debris, there was an orange light beyond the end of the woods, which seemed to hover like a dense curtain. As I flew closer, I could feel heat. I saw the raging flames just at the edge of a clearing. The flames popped and crackled and with a great rumble broke the silence of the sleeping forest. I flew in close, but the heat knocked me to the ground. I raised myself up and flew toward the light. My desire to leave the forest only strengthened as I met the fire. The dense smoke made it impossible to fly.

Determined not to return to Greshen Pond, I perched on a small branch. I could see the rage of the conflagration and felt the intense change happening to the forest floor. Just then, a rustle below captured the sound of the night. It moved quickly through the debris and disappeared along the edge of the fire, a long slithering body. I gathered my strength, lifted off my branch and dove down through the haze to land quietly on the back of the snake. His textured scales felt strong and weathered as he moved quickly around the burning ground. The smoke was so thick it was impossible to breathe, so I held on. He darted and moved quickly out of the forest, leaving the smoke-filled haze. I felt the coolness of the grass as the land transitioned and became soft.

I'm not sure when I fell off my travel companion, but I awoke to a light rain dripping softly onto the ground illuminating a spider's web just beyond me. I made a quick breakfast out of the web's occupant. Still a bit dizzy from the smoky air, my wings lifted me over the grassy hills below. I landed softly on a thistle, its lavender petals supporting my small body. As my wings surfed the air, I noticed my slightly torn back wing hadn't impeded my journey.

I had made it through the Denzund Forest! I flew into a wide-open field with rustling grasses and abundant black flies. My wings felt light, and I came upon the sparkling waters of a new pond. The water was cool and seemingly uninhabited except for frogs and other dragonflies. With no starken in sight, I landed on a pink lotus and thought about the parts of the forest I had flown through. Facing the fearful darkness had delivered me to this new home and my wings had supported me. I rested here in the safety of deep slumber.

Trena & Florine Duffield

Trena Duffield

Florine Duffield

Trena Duffield

I was born an introvert. Life's demands required me to perform as an extrovert. Silently observing human behavior, equipped me to evolve into a presence that was easily recognized as someone who could verbally crush you with the truth. This was my protection for interacting with the world.

On my 18th birthday, I showed up in NYC with only a toothbrush in my back pocket and $17, to be with my mentor, my beloved older sister Florine. We devoured all the opportunities of the Big Apple: acting classes, education, culture, and entertainment. We sought out influential people to develop the life skills we desired.

With entrepreneurial intent at the age of twenty-seven, I returned to Colorado to establish my own restaurant/bar. The "Cheers" ambiance kept my clients returning for 26 years. Then I sold the Joint.

Now I could do what I wanted. Realizing I possessed the power and ability to connect and serve others, I chose venues where my skills were highly valued. I volunteered through AmeriCorps, teaching life skills and ESL (English as a Second Language) to immigrants from Myanmar.

Now retired, I am finally able to return to the comfort of being an Introvert.

Florine Duffield

"I am not ready for the trash heap yet.
'Retire?' Why would I retire – I love what I do."

My art career started in the 1960s in New York City.

Humans, pets, wildlife, plants, and still life are my favorite subjects. I thoroughly enjoy creative writing and teaching art workshops.

Headshots are in great demand. Posing and showing their best features helps people feel confident about themselves. After a light retouching – amazing!

Painting oil portrait commissions, I sometimes work using photographs sent by clients.

Also, I travel to various locations making 'Destination Portraits.' After our photo session, we chose the best images for the painting.

My work has been exhibited in the US, UK, private collections, rec centers, Sky Harbor Airport Museum, Scottsdale Artist School, and the Association Gallery in London.

I reside in Arizona, with a gorgeous work studio that accommodates both painting and photography.

The studio assistant is Max, my 35-year-old Blue & Gold Macaw. One day, distracted by a phone call, Max flew from her nearby perch and landed on my palette which was loaded with oil paint. It took me two hours to clean her precious feet.

http://FlorineDuffield.com
https://www.FlorineDuffieldArt.com

Follow
LinkedIn: http://linkedin.com/in/florineduffield
Instagram: http://instagram.com/florineduffield
Facebook: https://facebook.com/fduffield
Phone: 623.565.0605

To watch our video interview with Florine, scan the QR Code with your smartphone or go to: https://youtu.be/1I1jnHQv3jw

A Tail in Two Cities

A Feline Fable, as told by Cyndi

Written by Trena & Florine Duffield, Sisters
"When I was young, I was afraid I would bore others.
Now that I am older, I am afraid they bore me."
—*Lee Marvin (Trena Duffield)*

"My actions are my only true belonging.
I cannot escape the consequences of my actions.
My actions are the ground on which I stand."
—*Thich Nhat Hanh (Florine Duffield)*

A Tail in Two Cities

Written by Trena & Florine Duffield, Sisters

*D*own and out in Dallas, I was on the streets, picking through trash, looking for something, anything. I had not eaten in days. The prime feeding spots behind the eateries were ruled by the alpha males. The leader of the pack was a one-eyed, dog-eared tabby, aka Rex, who bellowed, "This ain't no place for a defenseless little girl. The park's where you belong. Beat it."

Arriving at the park, "Yeow, sweetie, you look like you could use a helping paw," I heard her southern drawl.

There was 'Alma,' a maternal moggy with a sagging pouch.

"I'm starving and scared," I sobbed.

After a satisfying meal, I licked my whiskers, gave Alma a rub of thanks, and yawned. Alma led me to her safe sleeping hideaway. I curled up into the cradle of her warm belly.

My spirits were lifted. Alma said, "You need some learnin' if you wanna survive the streets. This ain't no barn dance." I graciously accepted her kind offer.

Alma stretched and jumped right in. "First, stay away from humans, dogs, and cars. Always plan your escape routes and hiding

places. Most important, during the day beware of animal control –
they will lock you up. Now, let's find us some grub."

One day, out in the open, we were spotted by the dreaded
animal control. Alma shrieked, "Run for cover!" and scampered to
safety. On the other paw, I froze. They had me!

Once inside the van, surrounded by other unfortunate felines,
I heard a voice, "Shelter ain't bad, just a pause, with grub and cover
to boot."

Upon arrival at the shelter, we faced the indignity of being
thoroughly examined. Goodness, all that poking and testing. They
removed my lady bits and snipped off the tip of my ear. I was officially
branded as a neutered stray.

The nights were filled with tales of past bonds, of freedom
tasted and lost, of families left behind or escaped from.

"I had to get out of that madhouse full of brats, always pulling
my tail, dressing me up like a baby, and recklessly grabbing me,"
complained the mixed breed.

"You think you had it bad," chimed in another captive, "I was
left alone all day, not allowed outside. They petted me mindlessly
while watching TV. What kind of life is that? I was enjoying life on
the streets, being free, now this!"

The beautiful Angora joined in, "I was always pregnant, nursing;
was nothing more than a kitten factory, until I was all used up. I was
a victim of breeders' greed. So, here I am with y'all."

The scruffy cat, "Where the heck am I? Animals should not
be indoors. I was quite happy in the barn, catching my own meals;
sleeping when and where I chose. I wandered too far from home, cars

all around, out of my element. A gentlewoman managed to get me in her car and brought me here."

My turn, "My family lost their home. Their new apartment did not allow me. Feeling unwanted; I took off. Not being street-savvy, I was snatched."

A voice of experience reached out, "Great stories. Let me tell you newby-cats what to expect tomorrow. The humans will browse until they find a cat who tickles their fancy. Once chosen, the humans will play with you. This is your chance; meow, purr, and rub your scent on them. They eat this up."

The next morning, several people wanted to handle me because of my charm and youthful appearance. I got many 'oohs and ahhs' but that was it. After several days I heard I had not been chosen because of my dental woes.

Another cat who was not chosen confessed it was because he was skittish and did not present himself well. "They are shipping us unadopted to a shelter in Denver because we are over capacity."

Shur nuff, the next morning we were sedated for the long journey. When we sobered up, we were at a new shelter. The air felt different. Same routine, different cage.

A day later a woman with silver hair seemed quite keen. The staff member filled her in on all my particulars. The bit about my toothy troubles did not deter her. She simply thought I was purrrrrrrrfect! How about that! She sprung me at once. I felt scared and elated at the same time about the uncertainty of my destiny.

When she took me to my new home, a tender old woman named Cyndi, welcomed me with her warm lap. She immediately named me Cyndi's Cat! I loved being cherished once again. It was quiet, with plenty of toys, delicious food, and treats – heavenly. I had all the attention I wanted. We did not leave these rooms. Other humans brought her food three times a day. Sometimes we had visitors. I usually hid till they left.

A cruel stroke of fate took Cyndi away. She had broken her hip. I never saw her again and was all alone.

'This house is maintained entirely for the comfort and convenience of my cat,' the plaque on the front door read. I love this place already. The first thing I smelled was another cat.

"It's okay, sweetie, you're safe now," my new mom kissed me and gently put me down. The downstairs bedroom was prepared with food, water, and my own litter box.

"Come up when you're ready." Then she went upstairs.

I looked around and found a place to hide and sleep.

The next day, I ventured slowly up the stairs. I met the rest of my family: BC, the 18-year-old, all-black shorthair, alpha tom (I called him the "old man"); the husband of the house was called Dad; and of course, my Mom.

I observed the most curious scene, my mom bent down, talking to the old man, who waited patiently.

"Would you like your breakfast, darling?" He meowed and meowed. "How 'bout some salmon bisque"? she asked, shaking the pouch. Again, he replied, watching her put his bowl down.

She extended a second bowl, bent down, and whispered, "This is for you Cyndi" and put it on a different rug meant for me with water and dry food. Goodness, what a feast.

The patio door was open; Mom and Dad were outside reading at the table. The old man was drinking and paw-splashing in a huge water bowl. I approached him from behind, sniffing his tail.

"Knock it off, toots," he hissed and continued drinking. We kept our distance.

That night, "This is just for you." Mom, in her soft voice, "We are a lot alike. I sometimes need a quiet, hidden place to collect myself and relax." She carried me to a blankie bed deep within her walk-in closet in the room where the whole family slept. I quickly fell into my kitty dreams.

The old man gradually realized I was there to stay.

I followed him around outside while he did his perimeter checks.

"As head of security, it is my job to do checks twice a day. I am tired and physically unable to perform up to my usual standards. You would be the perfect replacement. I will train you." The old man explained.

The part I liked best was basking in the sun on the front stoop watching the neighborhood activities.

The old man warned, "Stay away from the street, other animals, and humans. When I was your age, I was the alpha tom. I have battle scars to prove it. I got smarter and learned life was easier when I avoided confrontations. The safest place for us is the fenced-in backyard.

In my spare time I continued to catch moths, grasshoppers, and dragonflies, gifting them to my family. I loved playing in the backyard. Mom and Dad frequently joined me. Dad enjoyed a thrilling game of hide and seek. He laughed uproariously when I won.

"You found me." Humans are easily amused, I thought.

The old man continued my training as he grew noticeably weaker. It was announced that he was officially retired, and I was the new 'head of security.'

I loved having a job. I enthusiastically performed my checks twice daily.

Happy hour began around three. I jumped into Mom's lap and she hand-fed me a chicken treat. Then it was time for snuggles and settling down for the evening. I was always the first one to retire and the last one up.

Everyone was pleased with the new family dynamic. Mom and I continued to communicate. Our home was filled with laughter and caresses.

Living like a queen, I quickly gained weight, now a healthy eight ½ lbs.

Life is grand in my 'fur'ever home.

Chapter 6

Jeanine Robinson

I was the first-born of five children, and it seems my whole life has been about taking responsibility.

I was in such a hurry to grow up! I left home the day after school got out my junior year in order to run a small dairy bar owned by my parents. It was three hours away from where they lived. I managed that place for the entire summer. By the fall, I was far too independent to still live at home, so I changed high schools for my senior year and graduated early.

I was a licensed cosmologist for 30 years, but discovered my true passion was real estate. At age 50, I got my real estate license.

I continue setting new priorities in my life and am committed to enjoying the relationships that I am blessed to have. I'm planning to broaden my horizons by traveling more and worrying less.

I am so grateful to live in a beautiful area of northeast Arizona. I share my life with my husband, Eric, of 44 years, and our three children and six grandchildren.

~ Jeanine Robinson

To watch our video interview with Jeanine, please scan the QR Code or go to: https://youtu.be/cGc4VSxNukk

Dream Weaver

By Jeanine Robinson

*"You are the author of your own story.
Write the story you want to live."*

Dream Weaver

By Jeanine Robinson

Once upon a glorious time, an exquisitely beautiful girl named Lily Rose was born into the timeless era of Water. In this age of restoration, rejuvenation, and renewal, her otherworldly Ava-STARR's superpower was COURAGE. Her mission was to be strong in the face of danger, face fear as if it were already defeated and, most of all, be brave enough to be aligned with her aspiring intentions. She was supremely chosen to be a Dream Weaver.

In fact, her assignment of becoming a Dream Weaver obligated her to live by beautiful bodies of water such as black-inked oceans, turquoise glaciers, meandering creeks, inspiring inlets, wild rivers, peaceful ponds, and luminous lakes. She belonged to each of these mystical, watery ways of intrigue. Her depth of inner knowing confidently coursed its wisdom as her guiding compass in this journey of life. She was to become a skilled Way Shower to connect, cultivate, and consecrate the most sacred dreams of her fellow humans.

Lily Rose was sublimely blessed by her noble parents. They supported and understood her soul's purpose, so gifted her an early inheritance of their luminous Coral Castle by the Sea. Once she mastered her future, this celestial citadel was slated to become the classroom for her students, the next generation of Dream Weavers.

Upon receiving the keys to this luxurious new home, her violet blue eyes sparkled with joy. Lily Rose's perfectly symmetrical face was framed by her long, black hair, and she was a lovely sight to behold. Her wardrobe consisted of endless rows of gossamer gowns in cobalt blue, charcoal, moss green, Star Cerulean sapphire, tropical aqua, dark Pacific, and tidal wave teal, which seemed to flow like waves on the ocean. Her gowns produced a wonderful calming effect on all within her presence.

As an Initiate, one of her first Dream Weaver duties was as Gate Keeper. She had exclusive access to the profound portal leading to the magnificent Pearled Palace where all dreams go. Whenever Lily Rose passed into its sphere at will, she witnessed the benefits of having specific intentions. When their dreams, goals, and wishes arrived at the opulent Pearled Palace, the frequency vibration of each vision was spontaneously measured. The ones resonating with beauty, love, and gratitude were instantly sent into the Corridor of Fulfillment.

Lily Rose's mysterious, mythical, and miraculous Water Energy was one of five timeless elements. As such, she was higher in rank than Wood's creativity, Fire's passion, Earth's pleasure, or Air's synchronicities. Her highly evolved Ava-STARR's superpower held the COURAGE required to step in, step up, and answer the call of one's Destiny. Lily Rose found joy in embracing her spiritual purpose.

One of her favorite pastimes was to float peacefully down the River of Blessings on her back. During this tranquil time of contemplation, she expressed gratitude, knowing her life would be a series of opportunities to help others better understand their inner and outer soul growth. By elevating their sacred dreams, she could starseed the earth with Divine Love.

Thankfully, Lily Rose could also fast forward into the future. She adored observing the profound blessings of those who aligned with and accomplished their dreams, which impacted future generations. Their budding legacies were multifold. She also taught her students to be ever mindful of the gifts they received and honor the abundance created by possessing a willingness to share their gifts with others, so that they too could find their own luminous paths. Lily Rose's mission was to keep the dreamers and their dreams connected, allowing their dreams to become engaged, uplifted, inspired, and realized.

As a Dream Weaver, she called upon her ancient Dream-cesters to better navigate the ever-changing, now uncharted oceans she knew only too well. With her sincerity to serve from the heart, she was granted the ability to unfold, untether, and elongate dreams into even more elaborate visions. She continuously created a better tomorrow, today.

To bind to the soul a solid potential that already dwells within their spirit, she was given the gift of lifting the thin veil of the opulent Pearled Palace. With her talents, she helped nightly sojourners understand that the more they were truly aligned with their positive belief systems, the higher the probability was of manifesting their dreams. Little by little, night after night with consistent application, Lily Rose gifted bliss, benedictions, and exquisiteness to her dreamers. This process restored Dream Weaving. With Belief, initial obstacles were overcome which triggered the creation of a wonder-filled world of beauty, joy, and love. People saw one another with compassion, dignity, and trust. This not only raised the vibration of the planet, but actually lifted humanity.

Lily Rose, as a COURAGEOUS Dream Weaver and bold Gate Keeper, accepted the elegantly energetic responsibility of holding the sacred space of envisioning, activating, and living intentionally to bring about all that is good, wise, and deeply worthy.

The stages of life's journey were enhanced not only by dreams, but by the COURAGE to fulfill them. Creating peace and harmony on earth, one human at a time, placed her Divine Dream Weavers in alignment with the flow, and bestowed the ability to BELIEVE in Life's Infinite Blessings!

It is written in the ancient I Ching that those who are alert to their inner Divinity and know how to dream and believe will meet with great, good fortune. The Number One Hexagram denotes a time when the benevolent powers of the Universe are forever available to those who Believe. This Hexagram reveals that there is an unlimited outpouring of altruistic energy making profound progress possible for those who exemplify life's higher principles.

As a Dream Weaver and Gate Keeper, Lily Rose was attuned to what happens in a person's daily world, how their thoughts, words, and deeds directly impact their experiences. When dreams are suppressed, they become unexpressed. Shadow energy fuels fear, lack, and paralyzes a person to self-limiting beliefs. However, the watery essence of reflection, retreating and receiving expands the power of dreaming big dreams.

One of her greatest gifts is being able to visualize how far-reaching a drop of kindness can be. Like dropping a pebble in a pond, the rings of goodness continue to expand and bless other lives. What powerful magic this is! What an endless river of joy and self-awareness this creates! The magical lessons of letting go of ego and embracing joy, then helping others, is the straightest pathway to building a better life, not only for themselves, but for those who are also struggling to remember who they truly are and where they're from.

One of the most powerful methods of showing the luminous pathway was a beautiful bridge spanning a turbulent river. At the entrance to this bridge, the waters were very chaotic and turbulent. It took great COURAGE to begin this crossing, but by showing her dreamers how to navigate this bridge, she demonstrated that each step they took showed the river becoming calmer, and more peaceful. What a wonder this created! Not only crossing the bridge psychically, but by changing their intentions, they were building a pathway that left all past trauma behind. They were quite literally building a bridge and getting over it.

The other side of the bridge showed a stronger ancestral connection to peace, the power of COURAGE and intention, and how to manifest their highest and best life. As these advanced dreamers progressed toward a higher vibration, they were made aware of the desire to love unconditionally, recognizing that judgment comes from ego.

In offering a helping hand to those struggling with their journey, she helped them realize that we're all on the same journey, just on different paths. All paths lead to the same Source, which is Love and the Supreme Center. We are spiritual beings who chose life in mortal form, to learn specific lessons that require a human body.

Dreams open the portal to achieving our dearest wishes. The key to this portal is Love, which is also Light. We always attract what we are mentally and spiritually radiating. The more details we add to our dreams, the faster we can manifest them. These are the gifts and lessons the Dream Weaver leaves for all who have the COURAGE to find their own highest and best life possible.

Have COURAGE, dear dreamers! Darkness cannot exist in the Light. Dream your dreams. Express joy and gratitude. You will receive the keys to the magnificent Pearled Palace.

Chapter 7

Joan Smith

Who Am I?
~ Owner of My Life's Journey ~

Every day, we create our Heaven or Hell when we endure traumatic events in our lives. You can live in the pain and fear of your mind, or you can pray to receive the strength and fortitude from the God Most High, taking you on a new life journey within a new spiritual realm.

As God took me to a new and higher mind space
Like a Phoenix rising from the ashes
I Became Who I am Now

Manifesting My Life's Passionate Desires
Fulfilling My Creative Spirit
Becoming a Conduit
of Spirit's Love and Light Frequencies,
Bringing Beauty from the Inside Out
Making Elemental Changes in life's vortexes.

Joan Smith
Cell: 717-264-7272
Elemental Changes Feng Shui Consulting

Facebook for Inside Out Salon:
https://www.facebook.com/profile.php?id=100063674388946

To watch our video interview with Joan, please scan the QR Code with your smartphone or go to: https://youtu.be/I5fmbW-Pm7o

The Fire Within

By Joan Smith

"A heart filled with love is like a phoenix
no cage can imprison."
~ Rumi

The Fire Within

By Joan Smith

Part 1
Once Upon a Time

From deep in the womb of Mother Earth, floating in the river of pure bliss, I was softly awakened in the enchanted garden of Shambala by birds singing songs, animals communicating, and trees whispering words of wisdom. In a flash, a sonic boom — a shockwave sent from the Universe — was penetrating my soul.

A Phoenix rising from the ashes, I rose above the fear, sorrow and grief I felt from the imprisoned loneliness caused by the loss of my beloved griffon. Our souls were now severed in two, but with a promise of returning to each other in another lifetime, as my Twin Soul, GODZEUS, the Dragon of Heaven and Earth.

Only by this Divine Union could the "New Earth Paradigm" unfold.

As the Fire Within engulfed my being, the flames igniting my wings, illuminating my way through the darkness, I felt a freeness, a weightlessness being one with the infinite Cosmos entwining my fiery breath with the flight of dragons that surrounded me. Each beast possessed sacred chakra energy vortexes of power that I needed to consume so as to come into pure ascension with GODZEUS, the Yang to my Yin.

As I soared higher, Archangel Sandalphon, "he who serves the crown," merged into my energy field, also engulfing my being with life's frequencies. His feet were grounded into the earth, while his head reached into the heavens. His frequency released an elevated essence of my being, taking me to a 5-D sacred mind-space, igniting luminous directives. I was connecting with the infinite universe, becoming a conduit of enlightenment of human consciousness, a catalyst for profound change in this moment of time.

The Archangel of Ancient Wisdom, Metatron, granted me the Knowledge, which was once hidden, allowing me to receive the mental downloads of the sacred Akashic Records, the Book of Life and Remembrance; a "database" containing every thought, action, life experience and emotion from my past, present and future; occurring somewhere in space and time, with the potential to manifest my realities. I was now recalibrating, resetting and refining universal frequencies of "Divine Love."

I am One with the world and the Universe. I am the Phoenix, the FIRE WITHIN igniting my Goddess energy; conjuring what once lay dormant within me, now transforming from who I thought I was to who I know I am. I am the Divine Feminine manifesting my life's passionate desires, fulfilling my Creative Spirit, being a conduit of Love, Light, and Frequency, bringing Beauty from the inside out causing elemental changes in life's vortexes. I was born of Love's 528 Frequency. I am Hera~Gaea, Empress of Heaven and Earth. As Above, So Below.

Part 2
My Flight of Dragons

As I flew higher into the heavens, I was engaging in breathing exercises and frequencies with some of my beasts. I was feeling a very spiritual, physical and mental transformation. I was enjoying life with all my senses open. I could feel "all that feels."

The Dragons were teaching me that true transformation can only occur by making inner changes which create a positive mind space for self and the Divine, in which all possible relationships with others can flow. I knew there was no way to ascend if I made the same mistakes over and over, blocking my path to the next kingdom, leaving me in a stalled state of purgatory once again.

My Flight of Dragons increased as my feminine energy became a beacon of sensuality, unleashing a flirty, fun and playfulness I thought I had lost forever.

Fueling more of my Majikal Goddess — three dragons had pierced me with their fiery breath — I was feeling more powerful as I inhaled their flames of pleasure, entwining our energies together from lives past.

Each of my seven dragons had immersed me with their energy centers for the purpose of birthing the "New Earth."

Not one of my dragons possessed all seven portals I needed in order to fulfill my life's prophecy, but each one enlightened me in some way, whether positive or learning from the negative.

I was moving closer to a complete metamorphosis as "Hera-Gaea."

As each portal opened, I experienced a spiritual immersion of the greatest magnitude, purifying my body, mind and soul.

As I soared, each dragon led me to their sacred heaven, each one coming with another inner obstacle I needed to clear before advancing to the next higher realm. Each dragon's portal required me to detach from something.

Portal 1

Let go of negative family habits and behavioral patterns that cause a lack of stability and insecurity in the physical material world.

Portal 2

Release sexual guilt, shame and addictions.

Portal 3

Detach from anger and disempowering thoughts, the small ego.

Portal 4

Show forgiveness to self and others, let go of deep-seated fear.

Portal 5

Stop toxic language and poor communication, speak truth, listen and act with integrity, give thanks and gratitude.

Portal 6

Open up intuition, decision-making, purify my mind with divine thoughts, meditation and prayer.

Portal 7

Let go of depression and low energy, which prevent spiritual connection with self and others, as well as the Divine; this will release foggy mind, mental confusion, and headaches.

Love's 528 Frequency

I was now regenerating my DNA, living in Love's 528 Frequency, able to release old belief patterns from karmic pasts, transmuting them into learning experiences. I no longer bore the burden and anxiety of people and situations.

My Akashic Records revealed to me that I was to release all notions of how my mind mistakenly defined Love. As I started closing out these portals, I became the master of my destiny, opening up my true self to be filled with the "SPIRIT" of peace, joy and total fulfillment. Spirit told me that only then would I be granted a love like no other, with my Twin Soul, GODZEUS.

I felt a power of wholeness from within the Divine Consciousness. I was now experiencing a dimensional shift, traveling to a different realm but remaining in the same place, exiting the matrix and entering the New Earth paradise.

~~~~~~~~

Something was taking place as my Goddess Energy was raging through my being. THE FIRE WITHIN had ignited the root of my body, permeating a very sumptuous feeling of Utopia. Bregen, my Red Dragon, awakened the Kundalini energy that lay dormant, unleashing the sensual serpent within. This energy slithered through my chakras, one by one, the intensity rising from my tailbone to the living space of my mind. EVERYTHING was changing. Little did I know...

I was manifesting my soul's desire, my Divine Masculine, GODZEUS! I could feel his presence surrounding me. He was everywhere but nowhere.

Part 3
Letter to the Infinite Universe

My soul remembered a time where I, the Phoenix, and my Dragon Spirit entwined in each other's fire-breathing Ancient

Wisdom, infusing light, igniting the power of love, healing a world that was falling apart.

Being a conduit of Love and Light, my Empress energy started to heal mankind, I found complete Peace in just Being. The Divine cloak of protection surrounded me as I grew stronger.

~ To My Dearest Gentle Beast, GODZEUS ~

As the winds of heaven dance between us, I can feel your benevolent, imperial power wrapping around me with such softness yet hardness, your fiery breath unleashing inside me, feeling submissive yet empowered.

Your love envelopes my soul. My life force is in complete rhythm with your divinity. I feel our hearts pounding wildly together, feel you entering me as I enter you. Our senses are ONE, vibrating on such a high, on Love's 528 Frequency.

Deepest Love from your Phoenix,

Hera Gaea

~~~~~~~

As I put my letter to GODZEUS out into the Infinite Universe, suddenly I am being vacuumed through the Dragon's 7th Portal, now traveling through the 8~8 Lion's Gate. I am now launched into the 8th realm, where our energies first collided.

As I was entangled with my GODZEUS, I looked directly into your dragon eyes. That moment of familiarity was when I realized that we were mirroring each other's souls once again, my Twin Soul, GODZEUS, my Divine Masculine.

THE FIRE WITHIN

And so it was written throughout
all the land and Universe

Empress Hera-Gaea and Emperor GODZEUS entwined into the heavens for eternity, unleashing vibrational love to every creature big and small, changing the world into the "NEW EARTH." The love of the Dragon and Phoenix energies together would create Peace, Harmony and Joy for all humanity for eons.

NEVER THE END.
JUST A NEW BEGINNING.

Chapter 8

Jody Sharpe

Award winning author, Jody Sharpe, had a rewarding career as a special educator. Writing about angels became healing after losing her daughter and then her husband. Sharpe learned valuable lessons about moving forward and loving life in the now. Her stories about angels are written with love, humor and spiritual awakening. The fictitious town of Mystic Bay she created has given her an avenue to put characters and themes together hopefully moving the reader towards contemplation of the precious life and memories we are given.

20 Moon Rd. An Angels Tale, her novella, won first place this year in the National Federation of Press Women communications contest.

Books By Jody Sharpe
Mystic Bay Series:
The Angel's Daughter
To Catch an Angel
Town of Angel
Town of Angels Christmas
20 Moon Rd. An Angel's Tale

Special Needs Children the Angels on My Shoulder
Summer of Angels - a mystery
When The Angel Sent Butterflies - a children's book

Jody Sharpe's stories not only honor her late daughter and husband but her family, friends, and those who kindly share with her their own personal angel stories. She believes that we never walk alone.

Sharpe is available for speaking engagements.

Sharpejody76@gmail.com
www.jodysharpe.com

To view our video interview with Jody please scan the QR Code with your smartphone or go to:
https://qrco.de/JodySharpe

The Night Bird
& The Angels

By Jody Sharpe

"Amid the raindrops and sunshiny days of my life's journey,
the angels have always been by my side."

The Night Bird
& The Angels

By Jody Sharpe

Once upon a time when I was a little girl of nine, on a warm summer night I had a dream. It seemed so real to me then. I remember I was sleepy and had pulled the covers up. I laid my head on my pillow as I said goodnight to Dukie, my fluffy dog. He was lying in his cozy dog bed.

Just as I closed my eyes, I heard the night bird's singing as I did every summer evening. I had never seen him, but I loved his song. His song stopped but then I heard the voices of children playing.

Curious, I got out of bed and ran to the open window, peeking out to see who could be there. I didn't see anyone. All I could see was the bright moon and stars twinkling in the sky. The night bird began to sing again, high in a tree. I knew at only nine that I was never supposed to leave the house at night. But I had to find out if I had heard children. I took my pink doll blanket. The light in the kitchen showed us the way as Dukie followed me tiptoeing down the stairs.

Now that years have gone by, I finally remember the night clearly. The night bird stopped singing and I heard children's voices again. Who could they be? I stopped. Unlocking the creaking back door, hoping my parents couldn't hear me, I peeked out, but I couldn't see anyone.

Dukie happily ran down the steps. I felt brave and followed yet I couldn't hear any children's voices anymore, just the night bird's sweet song above.

My enchanted backyard forest's tall trees and bushes swayed in the summer breeze. I thought the moon looked as if it was shining just for me. I smelled the lilacs.

Crickets lulled me as a plane passed high above. I sat down by a tree I loved to climb. Sitting on my doll blanket, I put Dukie on my lap and stroked his head. I looked up at the stars. Resting my head on the trunk of the tree, I closed my eyes.

I must have fallen asleep because I woke up hearing children's voices close by. I opened my eyes to see three children sitting cross-legged beside me. I rubbed my eyes but could see them because the moonlight was shining on their faces. Could this really be happening?

I wasn't afraid because I used to play with the three children back when I was four. The little girl and two boys went away one day. I remember asking my mom where they could have gone. But my mom shook her head, never believing they were real. She said, "Justice, they are just your imaginary friends." I was sad, to me they were real.

Excited now, I wondered could they be here to play with me.

"Do you remember us?" asked Rachel. She had big brown eyes and dark hair like me. I remember she loved to dance in a purple tutu.

"Yes, you're Rachel. I remember you, Tobias and you, Joshua. I haven't seen you since I was little."

Tobias nodded. "We are here again to show you something you'll remember a long time from now."

"My mom said you're just imaginary friends."

Rachel laughed, "I promise, we are real."

Tobias said, "Remember how we played hide and seek all afternoon?"

I remembered. "Yes, it was fun."

"But we're not imaginary. We are really here and with you always. Justice Sage, now that you are nine, we will tell you who we really are. We are your guardian angels sent from heaven."

Surprised, all I could say was, "You are angels?"

"Yes," said Rachel smiling.

"I never saw an angel except in books and my dad plays songs about angels at Christmas."

"You believe us?" Tobias asked.

"Yes. But where are your wings?"

"Joshua said, "We will show you our wings later but now we will show you the future then we will fly away."

"Don't go," I cried.

"Don't cry please. People are coming in your life and will bring you happiness. Come with us down this path through the woods and see the future, a future with angels by your side."

After I wiped my eyes, Rachel and Tobias took my hand. Dukie followed close by. My enchanted woods were quiet as we walked but became lighter as the trees had strings of stars attached to the branches. Even the moon was shining brighter. I watched Dukie look at them and knew he saw them too.

We stopped by a big tree and there I saw a teacher talking to a classroom of students in the woods. She was speaking to a teenage girl who I somehow knew was me in the future. My hair was long, and I smiled at the teacher.

Rachel said, "You see yourself in the future. Your teacher is really an angel. She will give you a chance to volunteer with some little girls with special needs because you have a helpful heart for others."

"My teacher's an angel?"

"Yes," smiled Rachel.

I loved looking at the teacher and me in the future and didn't want to walk away. Joshua picked Dukie up. Suddenly our steps didn't touch the ground anymore. We were floating above the earth. The three angel's wings burst forth like parachutes colored with sparkling snow. We floated over a little stream. By the bank there was another classroom where I could tell I was all grown-up and the teacher of my own students. I was smiling.

Tobias said, "You will become a kind teacher yourself one day." Again, I didn't want to leave. I wanted to just look at the little students, but the angels urged me on.

We came to a clearing. The moon was higher, the meadow shining with moonlight as bright as sunshine. I saw myself as a grownup sitting on the ground hugging three little children, two girls and a boy.

Rachel said, "One day you'll have three children." I wanted to go to the children, feeling so much love for them. A tear fell down my cheek. Tobias said, "You'll love being a mother."

We moved on. I wanted to stay with my children but the image of them slowly disappeared. I saw a tall man with gray hair standing with me. He was talking to me, but I couldn't hear the words, but I knew I was sad.

"Who is he?"

Joshua said, "He's an angel who came to help you when you were sad. You will remember him all your life and decide to write books about angels because of this angel."

I wanted to ask why I'm sad, but I felt my feet lift higher. My hand was holding Rachel's and Dukie was flying in Tobias arms. I felt like my night bird must feel soaring over the treetops.

I looked down and below. In the meadow dogs and cats scampered around playing. All the animals stopped and looked up at us.

Tobias said, "These are the animals you will help in the future. You will love them dearly and they will love you. You will rescue many animals, insects, and birds."

I wanted to fly down to pet them, but I knew I couldn't. I looked back at them as we went on sailing in the summer night. We came to the edge of the meadow and Rachel gently told me, "You will forget what you have seen tonight but you will always remember we are your guardian angels. Now it's time to say goodnight."

"No, I want to stay with you and keep flying," I cried out. I want to go back and see my children, my animals, my students and my teacher again!"

Tobias said, "Justice, remember, we will always be near."

It's then my eyes closed. I tried to open them. I heard the night bird singing and my eyes opened. I found myself back in my bed with Dukie.

"Come back," I called, running to the window with Dukie in my arms. We saw them fly with shimmering wings, "We love you," they called."

The angels flew higher into the night till I couldn't see them anymore. I sat down on the floor hugging Dukie. My tears fell, I wanted my angels to return. I tried to remember the scenes from my future. I only remembered my three friends, my angels.

I held Dukie close whispering, "I'll take care of you and love you forever."

I remember that night vividly now. Looking out the window, I saw my night bird high on a branch singing just for me.

From far away, I heard them call, "Remember!"

Long ago my angels showed me my future. Truly, between the raindrops of my life, there has been sunshine and joy.

"Thank you, Rachel, Tobias and Joshua," I whisper as I sit down to write more angel stories. As always, the night bird begins to sing.

Chapter 9

Julanne Dalke

Student of life, Julanne Dalke is a writer committed to helping others find freedom to follow their faith-based path. She is also a professional voice actor, painter, and meditative studies class facilitator. Her company, *What's Your Story,* preserves audio publications that honor and celebrate individuals by listening to and preserving their stories.

Julanne holds certificates of education in the fields of meditation, writing, and public speaking. She writes, directs, records, edits, and submits audio recordings for a weekly radio show for Recreational Reading for the Blind, Phoenix, Arizona, and holds a certificate of over 5,000 hours for outstanding service from Katie Hobbs, Governor of Arizona.

Julanne is the facilitator and founder of *Free to Be* for in-home meditative studies.

Julanne has written and delivered numerous speeches and holds many awards for exceptional achievement in the Toastmasters International Communication program.

A strong relator, Julanne specializes in the area of encouragement. She allows the spirit of increase to express itself through prolific writing. Julanne believes as you learn to trust the wisdom of your heart and make creative choices based on what you know to be true and right for you, the process becomes progress.

CONTACT INFO:
julannedalke@yahoo.com
julannesmusings.blogspot.com
http://www.vfademos.com/JDalke
LinkedIn: https://www.linkedin.com/in/julanne-dalke-484a904

To view our interview with Julanne, please scan the QR Code with your smartphone or go to: https://youtu.be/Vw_pNFkYu7s

The Mourners

By Julanne Dalke

"Make yourself familiar with the Angels,
and behold them frequently in spirit.
Without being seen, they are present with you."

~ St. Francis de Sales (1567 – 1622)
Saint of the Catholic Church, Bishop of Geneva

The Mourners

By Julanne Dalke

The angels Gabriel and Othello perch on top of the roof at St. Agatha's Catholic Church to begin a training session on the art of ushering one into divinity. A long black hearse pulls up to the curb.

"What's all this about, Gabriel?"

"Catholic funeral," Gabriel explains. He is training Othello in the art of helping the deceased person to pass.

"Someone very special has died and their mourners have come to pay their respects. We will keep an eye on them throughout the processional. Pay attention."

"Is it a celebration?" Othello asks.

"Sort of. It's often a sad event, but family and friends gather together, eager to see one another, show off their kids and reminisce. It's a celebration of the deceased person's life, as well as an opportunity for families to get together again who may not see each other for years."

Children play, oblivious to the quiet chatter. Dressed in Sunday's best they look dapper, even though trousers are baggy from big brothers' hand-me-downs. Neckties are too long, and crisp white shirts are buttoned incorrectly in mother's haste to get the children ready and to church on time.

In observation, Othello raises one eyebrow and says, "Take a look at those kids' faces. Isn't that something? They show none of the grief of their parents but are overjoyed to see their cousins again."

Nodding in agreement, Gabriel says, "It would be nice if the adults could remember what it's like to be a kid."

"Are they European?" asks Othello. "Looks like an Austrian and Irish mix. Dark hair and freckles, hazel eyes. Did you say that was a Jarmer legacy?"

"Yeah, they're mostly Jarmers alright. Catholic immigrants from Austria who settled in Kansas. Most of the families attending today haven't met each other. Heck, this church probably holds four, five hundred people and it's filling up fast! Mae, the deceased, was married to Louie, who was the oldest of the thirteen children parented by Louise and Felix Jarmer. As a young wife, Mae left Kansas and followed Louie before the youngest of Louise and Felix's tribe were born. There's a twenty-year span between Mae and the youngest child born to Louise and Felix, the firstborn. And they live in two separate states.

"Louie and Mae were part of the firstborn children to leave Kansas for the luscious landscape of Oregon. Tragically, Louie died mowing the lawn at the age of 43. He left Mae with four children, nearly raised. Of course, they grew up and had families of their own, while Grandmother Louise still had two in diapers on the family farm in Kansas. Senior raised Holstein cows for the milk. Most of the older kids stayed in Kansas. The younger ones moved out west when the call for greener pastures became too strong. The family separated and created two legacies between Kansas and Oregon. Thus, the family split. It's complicated, Othello."

"The adult cousins seem to look at each other like the second family has no right to be there honoring their grandmother, " Othello says. "Offended, they would rob them of their private grief?"

"People will always be people," Gabriel sighs with regret. "These folks may be related by blood, but they don't know each other. As Mae's guardian, it's my job to see this thing through. Usher her soul into eternity."

Looking over the rooftops, Gabriel peruses the neighboring houses built at the turn of the century at the same time as St. Agatha's was built in the neighborhood. In those days, parishes were formed in primarily Catholic neighborhoods. Now converted to apartment housing, some are four stories high and take up half a city block. The church itself is massive.

"Othello, the Abbey stands firmly built with one granite stone upon another. It serves the community with distinctly Catholic significance and houses the clergy. Spires, arched windows, stained glass and liturgical Stations of the Cross are in every Catholic sanctuary. A portable cyclone fence surrounds the blacktop area that can be dismantled. It serves as a parking lot on Sundays, and doubles as a recess playground for the adjoining Catholic school. Children attend school Monday through Friday. Since today is a weekday and children are still in school, the mourners park on the street hugging the city sidewalk."

The bell tower sounds. Clang. Clang. Clang.

Family and friends mill about, talking and smoking near the concrete steps. A man pushes the dark oak double doors open at the entrance to the sanctuary, an invitation that the church is now open to visitors.

"That's Father Brenner," Gabriel says.

"The priest?" Othello asks.

"Yeah. The one with the star-studded white robe, gray hair, combed straight forward with the neat bang."

"Sort of reminiscent of a monk, wouldn't you say?" Othello says, leaning back on his perch.

"Have some respect, Othello," Gabriel says. "The other two are priests also, but for the procession they're assuming the role of altar boys, assistant to the priest. The altar boy on the right is carrying a smoking brass ball filled with incense, signaling the beginning of the procession."

"Pretty strong smell, I'd say. So what happens next?" Othello asks.

"Watch." Gabriel replies. "You learn by observing."

The outdoor family encounter calms down. A reverent hush blankets the sunny winter day. The solemn procession begins. Extended family file into the church to take their place amidst polished pews. Six pallbearers are neatly dressed in suits and ties, each lapel garnished with a white carnation. Two by two, the pallbearers descend the steps of the granite cathedral to retrieve Mae's body from the voluminous black hearse entombing the casket where she rests in peace on puffy pink satin sheets.

Following the casket up the steps are the priest and his altar boys. They carry a large gold cross studded with precious stones. It gleams in the filtered light as they crest the doorway. An ivory cloth is draped over the casket as if it could provide warmth to the cold metallic steel. Music from an ornate pipe organ plays while an operatic singer begins *Ave Maria.*

The immediate family follows behind, keeping step with the music. They sway melodiously side by side, heads bowed. Their veiled faces are obedient to the mood. The rest of the mourners stand to honor them in deepest sympathy.

Father leads the Mass in prayer. A devout parishioner runs her fingers carefully over a strand of heirloom rosary beads. In unison, the mourners repeat the Hail Mary and Our Father prayers in penance for sister Mae's soul, purging it from the flaming depths of purgatory. Preparing her soul for the highest state, heaven.

"As tradition has it," Gabriel explains, "the Catholic will not likely enter the pearly gates until the sins of the soul are eased by the prayers of the Catholic family left behind on earth."

The interior of the church is enormous. The vaulted ceilings are supported by massive, curved beams of wood and stone. Ornately carved marble pillars grace the front of the church.

Stained glass windows of remarkable craftsmanship depict Jesus as a boy in the temple, teaching. Again, as a man with numerous children gathered about his feet. The sunlight illuminates the colors that tell the story. The hardwood floors are polished to a shiny glaze. They reflect bits of light, and shimmer like ice frozen on a winter pond.

The Stations of the Cross are made of carved stone, touched by an artist's paintbrush adding color and a lifelike appearance. The Stations reflect a series of fourteen statues arranged in numbered order on a path along which worshipers, individually or in procession, move in order, stopping at each Station to say prayers and engage in solitude. These devotions reflect a spirit of reparation for the sufferings and insults Jesus endured. Each bears the image of Jesus on the way to his death on the cross.

An angel of lifelike proportion stands watch at the front of the church. She holds a torch as if on guard at the entrance to the tomb.

Her gaze is on Jesus hanging on a cross, which is the centerpiece in this magnificent House of God.

"Is that supposed to be an angel?" Othello says.

"In the eye of the artist, I guess you could say that it is!" Gabriel smiles.

"The service is closing," Gabriel says.

Father is dismissing the mourners row by row. The congregation sings "*Where Eagles Fly.*"

"Touching." Othello exclaims.

"You may get wings after all, Othello." Gabriel assures him.

Once outside the church and into the street, cigarettes are lit, the children scatter, cousins embrace, smiles reappear. Uncles trade fishing stories and brag about golf. Grandmothers cuddle babies, eat pie, drink coffee and pretend all is well with the world.

"They're parting, with another promise of organizing a family reunion," Othello exclaims.

"Mission accomplished," Gabriel says. "Chances are the next time they meet may well be another training ground for a wedding or a funeral."

Chapter 10

Junie Swadron

Junie Swadron is a psychotherapist, accomplished author, playwright, international speaker, workshop facilitator, and professional writing coach who works with aspiring writers to become best-selling authors.

Junie has penned and published seven books, two this year (2023), while traversing her challenges with cancer: *Write Your Life II: Peace Awaits You" and "Write Where You Are: A Guided Experience for Those Who Dream of Writing but Don't Know Where to Begin."* She's been called both unstoppable and resilient.

Junie sees the therapeutic and the creative processes as one. "It is about accessing a special place within us where serenity, love, courage, and truth reside. It is from this place that we begin to know our true spirit. It is from this place we begin to heal."

Junie's philosophy is encapsulated in her motto: *"Your soul meets you on the page, and something shifts. You strengthen, and you begin to stand taller. Then, one day, you begin to notice that your voice on the page has become your voice in the world."*

Junie lives in Victoria, British Columbia, and shares her life with her husband, David Halliwell, a widely accomplished artist and musician. They are currently co-creating a musical called *Today*.

https://junieswadron.com/
https://getbook.at/junieswadron
https://www.linkedin.com/in/junieswadron/
https://www.facebook.com/junieswadroncreativecounselling
https://www.instagram.com/junieswadron/

To view our video interview with Junie and David, scan the QR Code or go to: https://youtu.be/qxBE1pBpFjc

Just Supposing

By Junie Swadron

"Your soul meets you on the page, and something shifts.
You begin to stand taller, and then one day,
you notice that your voice on the page
becomes your voice in the world."

Just Supposing

By Junie Swadron

This is a modern-day fairy tale with a happily-ever-after new beginning...

Imagine a woman, imagine a man both 70 years young, discovering true love in the most unlikely fashion... A Halloween dress-up music party that neither one of them had any intention of going to.

She: doesn't like dress-up parties...

He: Shy, but eventually declares: "What the hell - I'm not doing anything else tonight, why not?" He grabs a cowboy hat, his congas and guitar and leaves his home.

She: had settled herself onto the sofa with a big bowl of popcorn, content to watch a movie on this cold, blustery October night, but the annoying, persistent voice in her head was getting louder and louder, "Go to the party!" That's when she begrudgingly got off the couch and consulted her pendulum, which started swinging frantically, almost off its chain, in the direction of YES! "Oh, fine!" she rebelled, yet proceeded to remove her comfy flannel pajamas, dressed herself all in black, found a pink flamenco mask, and walked out the door.

They: did not meet at the lively music party. No, it was now 1:30 in the morning.

She: Astounded she stayed this late, walked out the front door to go home.

He: Retrieving his musical instruments to put in his car and go home was walking to the front door at the very same time.

He: Upon seeing the beautiful lassie, quickly blurted out: "You're not leaving, are you?"

She: Ah, yes, in fact, I am.

He: Extending his hand, in the most gentlemanly way, "Hello, I'm David (in a thick English accent - quite charming actually).

She: Extending her hand, in kind, "Hello, David, I'm Junie."

At this point, he asks her the most inane question a person could ever ask: "What do you do, Junie?"

Junie: Rolling her eyes, "What do I do about what?"

David: Looking directly into Junie's eyes, "What do you do about everything, Junie? Tell me, what do you do about everything?"

Junie: Sensing his uncanny sincerity and completely disarmed, stuttered, "Uhm... I don't know if I can t-tell you 'everything,' but if you walk me to my car, I can t-tell you something, I guess."

And the rest is Fairy-tale history and what all great folklore springs from.

After their first date, David collected a bunch of Junie's lyrics from a musical she wrote years earlier that were collecting dust in a drawer. He proceeded to compose the music for each of them and delivered the completed songs a week later!

Junie was gobsmacked by his talent, speed and passion. However, there was one song sheet that she had given him that she adamantly wanted back.

"But I've already composed the music for it," he lamented.

"Sorry, but it's not going into a musical. It's too personal, and that's that!"

Well, that didn't deter David. He wrote his own love song and sang it to her shortly thereafter:

Is this a Dream?

There's a new moon rising
A new tide turning
Fill me through and through
It's so tantalizing
So mistifying
But I found myself in you
How did you find me?

You're the something I've been missing
I was just existing
But now you're safely in
I'll let you carry me down stream
Is this a dream?
Is this a dream?

I just thought I'd mention
You have my full attention
I'm melting into you

And I'm confiding
That I'm implying
You are melting too …ooh
We are each other

This tender love is so healing
Nothing's ever been this true
Every day is more appealing
Cause I wake up wrapped in you
Is this a dream
Is this a dream
Is this a dream

So, what did Junie now do with the song-lyric-poem she took back from David? She used it to propose to him only four months later, and he said Yes! (Brief aside…On their first walk, he said, "Oh, by the way, "I don't do marriage." She said, "Well, I guess this is short-lived then, isn't it? I have no idea whether I would want to marry you, but you've just shut the door on that." Trying to regain his composure, He blurted out, "No, that's not what I meant!" They worked it out).

After the proposal, they put the wedding date to be a year hence, happily sent out the invitations and started planning. Well, Junie did. Was it John Lennon who said, "Life goes on while you're busy making other plans?" Well, I can't say life went on…I'd say life, as we knew it, came to a full halt. The entire world went into lockdown. They named it Covid 18.

It took over every city in every country worldwide and every man, woman and child were mandated to stay at home, get inoculated, wear masks, form their bubbles (who would and wouldn't live under the same roof), and were told, "Don't be seen in crowds anywhere or you could get arrested."

The date we had proposed for our wedding became our Engage-Ment to Be Party. We held it in a large outdoor park, 16 months later where everyone was asked to stay at least 10 feet away from one another. Few people did. Everyone wanted to hug - and so we broke some rules, managed to stay out of jail, and by the Grace of God, no-one got sick.

Then, when the pandemic was officially over and friends and family could travel again, Junie used the same poem she proposed to David as her love pledge.

On September 18, 2022, she stood facing her true love under the chuppah (canopy) and the beautiful banner that said, "Our Religion is Kindness" and in front of a beloved congregation, she spoke these words:

"David, My Beloved…

Supposing there was a love
That formed from pure depth
A love that knew no tears, no regrets
Supposing that love was given to you
What would you do?
Just supposing

Supposing the fear that burdened your youth
Was now replaced by gentle truth
And you were given the chance
To let go and be free
And God's grace opened your eyes to see
That this is a love for eternity
Just supposing

Supposing the love within your soul
Is unburdened now – You let go to feel whole

And the tears you shed were cleansed by laughter
Forever after
What would you do
Just supposing

Supposing you were lifted higher than ever
By a love from one who cares
Supposing you shared the dreams of a lifetime
With one who can honour your prayers
Supposing I offered my hand to you
What would you do?
What would you do?
Just Supposing..."

Junie continued...

"And that day, on Salt Spring Island, on the beach you often shared with your beloved daughter, Cat, I trembled at the thought of being brave enough to place before you these words... David, will you marry me? Yet, I did. Oh my God. You said Yes! You said YES!

And we've been together now for almost three years. And there has been so much laughter and dancing in the kitchen, composing songs and writing stories together, cooking yummy dinners and cozying up on the sofa with Netflix where I would inevitably fall asleep, and hosting gatherings with our most beautiful friends and family. And yes, yes, my love, there have been tears, yet beyond all troubles that come to all couples, we are here today, here we are to stay – in love, forever after, forever after.

David – your heart is as pure as gold.
Your talent surpasses anything I've known.
Your love is as pure as a mountain stream.
You are the answer to my every dream

You are the answer to my every dream
Yes, you, sweetheart, are my answered prayer.

I love you, David Michael Darling Halliwell"

And now David looked lovingly into his beloved Junie's eyes and recited:

Junie Darling Swadron...
You are my heart's twin.
My soul's echo.
You are the safe home
I have longed for
For so long.

You are my dance in the kitchen
My kitten playing in the curtains
My beautiful Saving Grace and
I love you so.

I will always honour your choices
Respect your wishes, and
Support you in your mission
To reach and help others

Your kin are my kin.
Your friends are my friends.
And though you will be mine forever,
You will always be free.

Be free...Be you...Be happy
Be mine forever

And they continue to live happily ever after. He, in his studio composing music or painting magnificent oils paintings on canvas.

You can find Junie in her studio writing books and coaching others to do the same, and you can find them both oozing joy in all their artistic collaborations. The latest is producing the musical, "Today" – the very one with that very song that started this entire happily ever after love story!

Chapter 11

Marlene Hoskins

Marlene was born in Germany to a German mother and American father. She spent her formative years living all over Germany and the United States, attending 13 schools by the time she graduated high school.

Marlene trained and worked as a licensed cosmetologist in two states for a short while. She was also a licensed color and image consultant, a secretary and caregiver.

She now resides in the Arizona White Mountains after 36 moves to three countries and ten states. Marlene is still attending the University of Life with countless books that educate her. At this stage of her life, she continues writing her blog, quilting, and reading every book she can get her hands on.

Blog: https://insearchofitall.wordpress.com/

View our video interview with Marlene by scanning the QR Code with your smartphone, or going to: https://youtu.be/1eBXPvkdEcw

Hilarity Jane Hardy

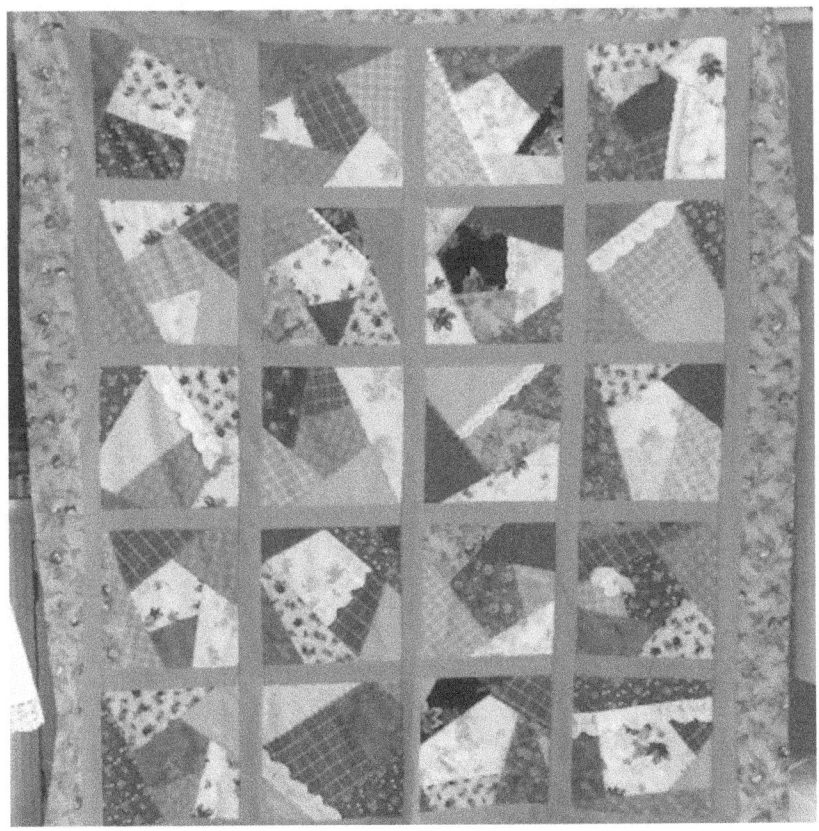

By Marlene Hoskins

"Laughter is carbonated holiness."

Anne Lamott (b. 1954)
Political Activist, Public Speaker, and Writing Teacher
Awarded a Guggenheim Fellowship in 1985
Inducted into the California Hall of Fame in 2010

Hilarity Jane Hardy

By Marlene Hoskins

Her mother had planned to name her Hillary Jane, but when the midwife who brought this huge toddler-sized child into the world saw her, she laughed out loud. She was also a bit tipsy on the Jägermeister that kept her going all night. Her exhausted mother asked what was so hilarious. She was quite angry that the midwife would be so rude before drifting into a deep slumber. The midwife was left to fill out the birth record since it was a home birth and decided to have the last laugh. And so, Hillary became Hilarity.

Growing up as a member of the Hardy family was not easy or fun. Postwar Germany left most without any humor unless they were in the Biergarten. Life was regimented and austere. Her German mother was the General in the house, and her American dad was the Sargeant. The kids saluted and did as they were told without conversation. The only Hilarity in their home was bottled up inside of her. Somehow, Hilarity knew her parents just didn't know any better. When her mother gave her a baby sister to take care of, Hilarity would talk to her gently, making her smile and giggle.

She made it her life's mission to bring as much laughter to the world as she could. It got her into a lot of trouble once she got into school, often leaving the classroom with tape across her mouth. It had to be removed before arriving home or there would be even more serious consequences. The teacher didn't appreciate her fanciful attitude about everything and disrupting the class with the silly remarks that just fell out of her mouth. She could never remember what she had said to make everyone laugh, but their laughter fueled her desire for more. It was like sunshine to her soul.

As the years passed, Hilarity continued finding so much of life joyless in her relationships with others. Only her children relished her whimsical nature. She would watch them play in the yard and read them stories every night. Her friends would come to visit her because they knew she had a kind and understanding heart and could see the light inside them. Life was often hard for them, too.

One day when the bottom fell out of her life on one level, Hilarity asked the Master Creator for just a little joy in her life. Her children were approaching adulthood and not around as much. She asked over and over for just a little joy. What did that look like?

Early one morning, a vision appeared before her in the form of a man named Homer. Hilarity looked up at the Master Creator and said, "Are you kidding me?" Obviously, the Master Creator had a ridiculous sense of humor, too. "For goodness sake," said Hilarity. "This man wears plaids and stripes together, has freckles everywhere, looks like an imp and I'd bet there is a point on the top of his ears! I don't even like him!" But then she heard, "He will teach you about joy even through hard times."

As luck would have it, it seemed they were both in the same difficult situation with life in transition making some very hard choices. Like him or not, Homer and Hilarity became a team. They worked hard making a stable home for the younger children still not quite grown. Hilarity taught his children the love of reading and storytelling. Homer taught her children how to use tools to fix and make things. Hilarity taught Homer that plaids and stripes only belonged together at home. Homer taught Hilarity what joy looked like.

Homer fell in love with Hilarity's laugh. He didn't have much of that at home either. His father was English and quite buttoned up and proper. Hilarity looked at Homer one day saying, "Your dad may be English, but there had to be an Irishman in the woodpile somewhere." Homer was very much not a "proper" sort of man and could do quite the impression of a human leprechaun.

Homer's mother was a farm girl in a big city. She loved to entertain and have ladies over for tea and cards. She'd been a cheerful woman until she lost her sight. Hilarity took over her care, as well as the children, finding ways to entice a smile or giggle from Homer's mother at each daily visit. Hilarity seemed to know just how to tease her. Homer's mom shared all her secrets with Hilarity and no one else.

Their first Christmas together was a sparse one. Gifts were essentials like shoes and sheets. They did get a real Christmas tree and put it up in the living room. The older children came by to help the younger children decorate that funny-looking tree. It was a joyful time. Then the tree fell over. Fear ran through Hilarity as she looked at Homer. What would he do? These kinds of things had always brought on catastrophic reactions in her prior life. Homer just looked at her and put the tree back upright. Nothing appeared to be seriously damaged.

As they were cleaning up the pine needles and tinsel, the tree fell again. Homer stood and then walked away. A few minutes later he returned with some wire, nails and a hammer. Homer proceeded to wrap wire around the top of the tree and with a swift jerk, raised it up. While Hilarity held it up, Homer tied the wire to a nail he put in the wall. The tree waffled a bit still, then went over for a third time, pulling the nail with it. Hilarity was trying hard to stifle a giggle. This tree had a mind of its own.

Homer took three more nails and hammered one into each of the three holes in the legs of the tree stand, right through the carpet! By this time, all the fear had left Hilarity, and she was rolling on the floor laughing. Who does this kind of thing? Who hammers nails through the carpet in the living room?

Everyone in the room erupted with a fit of giggles. Homer was looking quite proud of himself for having solved the issue and the tree continued to stand proudly all through the holiday. Homer suggested they leave the stand where it was for the next year's tree. Hilarity's sides hurt so much from laughing that she quit holding in the funny things that would often just fall out of her mouth.

That joy popped out in so many ways for Hilarity. She decided that life had given her so many scraps that she would learn to make quilts of them. They at least could be wrapped around those she loved and keep them cozy when she wasn't there to hug them herself. She never sold a quilt or made anything to order. The fabrics told her who the quilt or garment would be for and how to make it for them. She even quilted shirts. Her joy spilled over into so many creative endeavors that they were hard to contain. Everything she made was with love and joy.

Homer had taught her that you could have joy amidst the hard tasks of life. It wasn't one or the other. You could have both, even at the same time.

Hilarity had found her joy along with a lot of hard work. She and Homer continued to spread as much joy and laughter as possible for as many years as they had together. She still couldn't figure out where those funny thoughts came from and could never remember what she had said that caused such reactions. But friends loved to be caught in the fallout of laughter. A good belly laugh made each day worth living, no matter what else happened.

Chapter 12

Nicoleta Taylor

Nicoleta Taylor is an American author born in Transylvania, Romania, who moved to Phoenix, Arizona, in her forties. Her name reunites both her Romanian past and her American present.

Growing up in communist Romania, she found her refuge in reading and writing. At the age of 14, she won a popular Transylvanian poetry contest, setting a record as the youngest poet ever to receive such an honor. Later on, her writing skills gained recognition in the 1989 National Contest of Romanian Language and Literature, and the 2011 National Contest of Romanian Poetry and Short Prose.

On Earth Day 2022, she published her first poetry book, *Terrans: To MotherShip Terra's Stewards, with Love*, an Amazon bestseller in inspirational poetry dedicated to our planet, that intriguingly and insightfully coalesces science fiction with spirituality.

In 2021, she contributed to the collaborative book *Wisdom of the Silver Sisters - Guiding Grace* and in 2022 to its sequel *Golden Wisdom of Love Legends and Legacies,* both #1 Amazon bestsellers that added to her writing journey.

Nicoleta is also a licensed Romanian<>English translator, teaching Romanian language and culture to American students, and providing linguistic services for Duolingo, the world's most popular language learning app.

Blog: nicoletataylor.com
E-mail: nicoleta.taylor@yahoo.com

To view our video interview with Nicoleta, please scan the QR Code with your smartphone, or go to:
https://youtu.be/UGWgst91e4g

Umäni

By Nicoleta Taylor

"This free-will gravity,
drawing us together
and keeping us close
regardless of the time
and worlds between us,
is Love."

Nicoleta Taylor, "Love"
Terrans - to MotherShip Terra's Stewards, with Love
(2022)

Umäni

By Nicoleta Taylor

Glossary

Terra:	An alternate name for planet Earth, as well as the Latin name for the planet.
The Big Dipper:	Also known as the Plough or the Great Wagon; a large asterism consisting of seven bright stars of the constellation Ursa Major.
Alcor:	A binary star system in the constellation Ursa Major. It is the fainter companion of Mizar, the two stars forming a naked eye double in the handle of the Big Dipper asterism in Ursa Major.
Mizar:	A second-magnitude star in the handle of the Big Dipper asterism in the constellation Ursa Major. It forms a well-known naked-eye double star with the fainter star Alcor and is itself a quadruple star system.

Prologue

*T*hat summer night, the elderly woman sneaked outside her childhood home, built by her parents in a quiet Transylvanian village. She was barefooted and wearing her dearest nightgown, the white one with pink roses. The modest five-step stairs by the front door, made of plain concrete, were still warm, and she sat at the top, under the pale light of the new moon. She had been living far away for many years, across the Atlantic, in Phoenix, the mythical place where she started a new life in her forties, from the ashes of her Romanian past. This was her last trip to the place where she drank her first water in this Earthly life. "Terran, not Earthly," she clarified her thoughts.

Her family was peacefully sleeping inside. It was quiet, except for the gifted crickets singing their endless nocturnal hymns in the small rose garden at the front of the house. The power had been out for quite a while now, and the village was blanketed in a soft darkness. The unexpected blackout allowed the night sky to fully reveal its myriads of stars, with the Milky Way arching right above the house. But her eyes were drawn by the Big Dipper, just the way it had always been since she was a little girl and her mother first pointed it out. Her folk called it the Great Wagon, carrying the fate of humanity across the heavens.

"Count four stars for the wagon itself, and three stars for the pole to pull it. Can you see them?" "Yes," she nodded happily, her big eyes mirroring the wondrous lights above her. "Now look again," her mom incited her, "how many stars do you actually see in the pole?" She looked carefully, then counted on her little fingers, "One, two, three, four." "Where do you see the fourth one?" She decisively pointed her forefinger to the middle of the three-star formation. "Bravo," her mother praised her, "you have great eyes. Very few people can see the faint twin of that bright star." Oh, how proud she was of herself! Ever since, out of all of the constellations, the Big Dipper felt like her second home.

"First home, actually," she sighed, remembering. Her time to go back was drawing near and she longed for it, but her love for her Terran home felt stronger than ever. She caressed the spot on the cracked concrete where her mother sat so long ago, and wept silently, tears of bittersweet goodbye magnifying the gentle glimmers in the sky.

"I have to write, it's time," and at that thought Alcor, Mizar's twin, the dim star from the Big Dipper's handle, seemed to allow a glimpse into its full hidden splendor. "My sweetest one," she whispered, "I will see you soon." The wind brushed her face with a lock of the long white hair adorning her aged features and falling freely over her thin silhouette. After all these years, she still had the same big childlike eyes, marveling at everyone and everything. "Tomorrow...," she told herself, "...tomorrow... Until then, I will rest here for a little while and remember my here and my there."

Chapter One – Umäni

Let me tell you about my home world. I am Umäni, but this is not a name. It is a soothing echo, uum...maa...nee..., each syllable a gentle breath, out...in...out..., like a whisper of one's being. This is who we know we are when we think of ourselves, your distant selves, 83 light years away from Terra, your Earth.

We live under the lights of Mizar and Alcor, the double stars in the handle of the Big Dipper. But this is only the beauty that you can see with your naked eye. If you look at them with your inner eye, what you know as the bright Mizar is not one, but two pairs of stars: two bright dots like a punctuation colon, in the vicinity of another couple of bright dots like an oblique colon. What you know as the faint Alcor is also a pair of stars, a little bit further away, like a horizontal semicolon. They dance together across our skies, gravitationally bound to each other, and their gravity is love.

The Mizars rotate, taking turns in the spotlight throughout our evolutionary intervals. Each of them gets to be Um - uttered like the first breath - the central sun, which acts as our celestial logos, or the spirit of our world, under the wise guidance of its partners. We exist on Mä - like the first word - which is our home planet under the paired stars, hosting the celestial embodiment, or the physical body of our world. The same thing happens with the Alcors, that take turns being Ni - like the first gesture - the guiding star, our celestial psyche, or the soul of our world. Our Um-Mä-Ni Sources are themselves finite avatars of the same infinite intelligent Source and they navigate the universe as a star fleet on its awakening journey from the Source and back.

Therefore, we, the Umäni, are One, their embodied fractals, and in our world, there is no hierarchy, only cyclicity. We are each unique, like humans, and make a collectively conscious family of entities that evolved from what we think of as the T, the forest of our world. Yes... we used to be trees... hmmm...

Our communication replicates facets of the language of creation in a complex of sounds, feelings, visualizations, and channeling coded to reflect the building blocks of life manifested by the Source in the current octave of our evolution. We assemble these blocks, or units of meaning, to express what needs to be expressed, intuitively and naturally. They track the ascending spiral of creation, from the infinite Source to its Love awakening, to the creation of Light, and to its manifestations across evolutionary intervals of awareness. From Fire, Air, Water, and Earth as first-interval beings to Flora as second-interval beings, to Fauna as third-interval beings, to Umäni as fourth-interval beings, and so on and so forth, the language of creation guides and manifests us onward to the Source.

The intervals coexist and are interdependent. Those in the most complex interval are in service to all, which is the greatest honor. But service to all is service to our other selves on different legs of the evolutionary intervals, empowering our collective ascension as One.

Because of my Umäni ancestral memories, my English, just like the other Terran languages I speak, might sound odd to you now and then. They are becoming one in my inner voice, but it feels like breaking the rainbow into countless shards of colors and then describing them one by one. It is a fascinating and never-ending guessing game.

Now that you know where I come from, it's about time to tell you what I remember from my last life in the daylight of Um, the cradle of Mä, and the nightlight of Ni. What brought me so far away, to Earth, better said to Terra, is a long story...

With that thought, the woman rested for a moment her brown eyes with concentric gold rings, like the sapwood of old trees, obscured here and there by greenish spots, like young lichens. And somewhere, on the right pupil, a minuscule brown dot drew the shape of a tiny, winged creature, birdlike, or maybe angel-like.

To be continued...

Nicoleta Taylor is currently working on *Umäni* and plans to release the book in 2025.

Chapter 13

Norma-Jean Strickland

EXPERIENCE:

- Published PBS Television Emmy Award-Winning Celebrity Ghostwriter
- Published Author / Editor / Proofreader
- Producer / Narrator / Speaker
- Educator / Trainer
- Classical Musician / On-Air Radio Host
- Researcher with Expertise in the Arts
- Certified Assistive Technology Consultant for People with Disabilities

- Certified Paralegal (completed graduate work in law, with medical-legal specialty concerning disability issues)
- Bachelor of Music, Piano Performance (minor in Vocal Performance), Lifetime Performer
- Nationally Certified Writing Tutor
- Idea Generator / Education Pioneer
- Positive Change Activist in Support of Conscious Evolution

STUDIES:

- April 2023, Certificate, Navigating Pet Death, Centre for Sacred Deathcare
- June 2023, Certificate, Conscious Dying Coach, Conscious Dying Institute (CDI)
- September 2023, Completed, The Wisdom of Grief, Mirabai Starr and Caroline Myss
- October 2023, Pending Certificate, Pediatric Death, CDI

NJ's End-Of-Life guidance will focus on "Edge of Light." When you think of "Edge of Light," all you see is the beginning of radiance, which expands as you welcome the unknown. It doesn't have anything to do with physical death. It's about awakening inside when you dare to look.

Her new website won't be completed at the time of this book's publication. In the meantime, remember to look inside for everything. YOUR CENTER has all the answers.

CURRENT WEBSITES:
https://njstrickland.wixsite.com/starlightcreativepro
https://www.linkedin.com/in/normajeanstrickland/

EMAIL: njstrickland848@gmail.com

Watch our interview with Norma-Jean scan the QR Code with your smartphone or go to: https://youtu.be/kuKfs2EKJw0

Journey to the Center

A mirror never changes,
but everyone who looks
sees something different.

By Norma-Jean Strickland

"Ring the bells that still can ring
Forget your perfect offering
There is a crack, a crack in everything
That's how the light gets in"

"Anthem" song lyrics by Leonard Cohen
(punctuation omitted by Leonard Cohen)
"Anthem" was released in 1992, and conceived in 1984

THE IMAGINIST

CAST OF CHARACTERS

K	**Katanka**	I am Katanka, a TURTLE. I am ancient and and wise.
A	**Artie**	I am Artie, an artist.
L	**Lenny**	I am Lenny, the lens of the kaleidoscope.
E	**Echo**	I am Echo. I live in the back of the mirrors.
I	**Inkpot**	I am Inkpot, a RAVEN.
D	**Digger**	I am Digger, a BADGER. I love t0 dig to dig beneath the surface and keep focused on each moment. This is called THE ANY-NOW.
O	**Opal**	I am Opal, a HUMMINGBIRD.
S	**Squirt**	I am Squirt, an ELEPHANT. I'm associated with clouds, which are symbols of mist. They separate the formed from the unformed.
C	**Cascades**	We are the family of water droplets in the fountain. Our colors change depending on our moods and emotions.
O	**Otto**	I am Otto. I live in the front of all the mirrors.
P	**Palette**	I am Palette. I'm hidden inside the fountain.
E	**Eva**	I am Eva, a nickname for Evaporate. I'm responsible for clearing all the colors at the end of each day.

Journey to the Center

By Norma-Jean Strickland

It is dawn and the mourning dove is singing her distinctive song. The inhabitants of THE CENTER slowly awaken to get ready for their visitor.

Now that it's light, the water in THE CENTER fountain begins to move and circulate. The first one to arrive is Opal, who zips around the fountain briskly to summon the water droplets as they cascade from the top down. It is at this BETWEEN TIME when the droplets reflect the iridescence of Opal's wings to become all the colors of the rainbow that the visitor will see upon arrival. The fountain almost seems alive! As long as the water circulates, the colors the visitor sees remain vibrant.

Katanka lives underneath the water. He moves slowly because he is ancient. While Opal is rushing around, she doesn't notice Katanka has surfaced and is watching her from inside his shell. Katanka can feel the vibration of water with his sensitive shell, so he always knows when the others begin their activities.

Otto, Echo and Lenny have all awakened and have begun checking the mirrors they're each responsible for. Otto lives in the front of the mirrors. It's his job to keep them at the perfect angle to provide the most direct reflection and perfect symmetry when the color wheel is rotated.

Otto is a palindrome, so what you see frontwards and backwards is exactly the same. He likes everything to be balanced and in order. Whenever he gets a compliment, his favorite expressions are: "I'm just a mirror!" "Look in the mirror when you say that!" "I'm just a reflection of you!"

Echo lives in the back of all the mirrors and she's responsible for bestowing the colors with their backwards light, which creates all the pastels. Pastels are the reflections of all the brightest colors and Echo loves bringing them to life because they're really soft. When Echo speaks, her language comes out backwards, so it's difficult for the other inhabitants to understand. That's why everyone has to be very still in order to hear her. Squirt uses her sensitive trunk to interpret with sign language so that the others can comprehend Echo.

Squirt is young. She's still at that awkward stage and sometimes has two left feet, tripping down the walkway leading to THE CENTER fountain. She has never actually fallen, so all is well.

Lenny is the first character a visitor sees as they make their way down the long, dark tunnel of the kaleidoscope leading to THE CENTER. He keeps his lens sparkling clean and is constantly checking to see if there are any spots that might obstruct a clear view.

When everyone is finally awake and each doing their job to get ready for today's visitor, Inkpot decides to create some mischief. He quickly flies by the HALL OF MIRRORS where everything is angled perfectly, but he does so with the intent of spinning some of the mirrors out of alignment. He knows that everyone is busy working and won't notice these slight discrepancies, which is just what he's hoping for!

Meanwhile, Otto is coordinating the front of the mirrors while Echo is positioning the back of the mirrors so they can ensure that proper balance is maintained. This is necessary because every color must be seen since it has an important place in the overall vision of what a visitor will experience. Each mirror has its own unique place so the colors it reflects will shine brilliantly. If only one small mirror is out of alignment, it simply ruins everything, and Otto won't allow that to happen!

Squirt wanders into the courtyard where the fountain resides because she's looking for Opal. They usually play together, but only after Opal has finished her morning duties. The first thing Squirt notices is how beautiful and tranquil THE CENTER really is, even with everyone busily working.

Opal comes dashing over to Squirt and says she thinks they should look for flowers.

Now that Inkpot has shifted some of the mirrors, he flies to the end of the HALL OF MIRRORS and perches himself in one of the tallest trees. He can't wait to see everyone's reactions to the changes in mirror angles he caused. His feathers are so black, he virtually disappears into the shadows.

It doesn't take long for the chain of events to unfold. Some of the colors being produced by the Cascades aren't as bright as they should be. Usually, when they spill out over the fountain, they are dazzling, shimmering and almost vibrating with luminescence. However, some of the Cascades have started to fade and a few have even begun to turn gray!

This situation has now caught everyone's attention and Otto is particularly alarmed. "What are we going to do? What could be causing this? We have to do something before our visitor arrives!"

Meanwhile, Opal and Squirt have wandered out past the HALL OF MIRRORS in search of flowers, which are Opal's favorite things. They find a large meadow with every kind of flower imaginable, as far as the eye can see and Opal is thrilled! Squirt is so happy, she starts running to get there but is going too fast for her feet to keep up with her enthusiasm and she steps on her trunk!

This places her trunk squarely in the middle of several dozen flowers. As she takes a big breath to help pick herself up, she inhales the surrounding aroma deeply and immediately begins to sneeze, which causes her trunk to get all clogged up.

As Opal and Squirt make their way back to the fountain in THE CENTER, it becomes quickly obvious that something is terribly wrong. The Cascades in the fountain have become so sad and upset that they're not bursting into any colors at all! Virtually everything has come to a standstill!

Lenny thinks this is entirely his fault, so he starts cleaning all the glass in the huge lens and rubs so hard, it starts to squeak. No one notices that Echo is frantically trying to get everyone's attention. When she gets excited, her speech comes out backwards much faster than usual, which has now caused her squeaks to be overshadowed by the squeaking created by Lenny's obsessive cleaning!

Since Squirt understands Echo better than anyone, she approaches Echo as gently as possible, not wanting to sneeze again. Here in the HALL OF MIRRORS, that would be disastrous! After listening to Echo, Squirt takes in a long, slow breath so she can use her trunk to sign what Echo has been saying.

Unbeknownst to Inkpot, Echo saw him flying in the HALL OF MIRRORS earlier and knows that he's the one who changed the angles of the mirrors which resulted in the chaos that morning.

Relieved at learning the cause of the disappearance of colors, the others start adjusting the mirrors so that each piece fits back in its proper place. They still have time to finish before the visitor arrives!

Squirt is happy about helping Echo reveal what Inkpot did, but she still can't breathe. Opal makes a good suggestion. Since Squirt is the largest inhabitant of THE CENTER, her trunk should easily reach the sky. She stretches up as far as she can and her trunk finally reaches the clouds that are filled with refreshing mist. She inhales deeply, brings her trunk down out of the clouds, trots over to the fountain and pours the fresh water into the middle of it.

Harmony is restored!

Inkpot has been reprimanded and flies away from the fountain, his "cawing" laughter fading as he goes.

Opal got to play with her beloved flowers.

Squirt can breathe again.

Otto and Echo have all the mirrors in perfect alignment.

Lenny is sparkling with relief.

The Cascades are ecstatically happy and are freely flowing again with all their magnificent colors.

Katanka just smiles in his wise, knowing way and says to everyone:

"OUR VISITOR IS COMING!"

*****

Who lives in YOUR CENTER?

Chapter 14

Patricia Holgate Haney

Meet Patricia, a woman who has a deep connection to spirituality and a love for travel and adventure. Patricia's curiosity and thirst for knowledge have taken her to some of the most beautiful places on earth. She is a writer and avid reader of books, and her writing reflects her passion for exploring her own psyche as well as the world around her.

Despite her love for travel, Patricia is grounded by her family, who provide her with the support and encouragement she needs to pursue her dreams. She is always searching for new adventures and experiences, and she loves sharing her thoughts and insights through writing, as well as helping others pursue their own memorable adventures.

Through her writing, Patricia hopes she inspires others to embrace their inner adventurer and explore the world around them. She believes that travel is a transformative experience that can help us grow as individuals and connect with others in meaningful ways.

She has authored chapters in eight bestselling compilation books available and is currently working on her first novel. Let your imagination take you places that inspire you.

Join Patricia on her next adventure and discover the transformative power of travel for yourself!

https://www.amazon.com/author/patriciaholgatehaney
pholgatehaney@gmail.com

Website:
https://www.phtravels.com/

To view our interview with Patricia, scan the QR Code with your smartphone or go to: https://youtu.be/GbFdlPLgtEc

Journeys Through Lifetimes

By Patricia Holgate Haney

"The world is full of magic things,
patiently waiting for our senses to grow sharper."

W. B. Yeats (1865 – 1939)
Irish poet, dramatist, writer, and politician
Recipient of Nobel Prize in Literature in 1923

Journeys Through Lifetimes

By Patricia Holgate Haney

Kalpana gazed at the dark-haired girl lying on her thin blanket amongst the trees, where the angel light sprinkled through the branches, landing around her and softly lighting her face. She felt the girl's emotional journey.

Full of love, the girl had a look of wonder and longing in her eyes, yet she felt the sorrow and loneliness dwelling in her soul.

Curled up on the blanket, Grace tried to sort out her feelings. She felt alone, yet part of her felt a presence. She couldn't see it, yet she could sense it.

Sighing, she glanced up through the dark green foliage, watching as a cloud played peek-a-boo through the branches, barely touching the treetops as the clouds slowly traveled across the sky.

The leaves and needles rustled faintly in the breeze. Grace noticed the absence of the birds. They usually chattered incessantly, and she made up conversations to occupy her mind. Her imagination, at times, fueled her soul. Other times, it failed to be sparked.

Kalpana smiled. She could read her companion's soul, her thoughts. She had been with Grace for many incarnations throughout time -- the time that passed yet stayed familiar. Kalpana would be with her for all time.

Her purpose was to feed her charge's imagination, help Grace realize her worth, and value her soul. Help her find clarity. Her guidance was in her presence. Her help was not something that made a noise in the world. Instead, it was purely felt and heard within the heart and soul.

The road Grace had traveled was filled with hardship and yet also a sense of wonder. Strangers in strange lands, then strangers became friends. Sorrow, joy, despair, and hope all seemed to punctuate and color her journey.

Even harsh conditions, which sometimes seemed to push their spirits to the point of surrender, couldn't stop their mutual evolution. There was a purpose to the journey Kalpana and Grace shared. Promises of hope, beauty and bounty beyond imagination.

It was a long way from their generational homes in England. Strange lands, new customs, new people. New hardships.

Grace's father had told stories, which sometimes seemed unbelievable, for as long as she could remember. His words were vivid and eloquent. She could see in her mind all the people because the descriptions were so vivid. She could feel their pain because he explained it so well; she could sense their hopes and dreams. Her father didn't speak often, but his words were like magic when he did. He was a painter of stories, and she became a character in them.

Sometimes it was hard to tell where the stories left off and her life began.

Over the years, she learned to cope with reality by using her recollection of storylines and actions, making the mundane exciting and conquering fears and shadows by employing strategies she had experienced during her adventures.

When Grace finished her chores, her mother encouraged her daughter to "go talk to the trees for a while." She knew her daughter had an insatiable curiosity and an imagination that took her breath away.

Out of all the children, Grace was the one who listened wide-eyed to the stories that were told in family gatherings, breathlessly hanging on to every word. The first one to sit and listen and the last to leave. She wanted to know every detail, from the people to the locations. Her enthusiasm could be tiring, but her mother believed she would be the next storyteller, the traveler who carried their stories forward.

She smiled, watching as her daughter surreptitiously pocketed gifts for the fairies honoring myths passed down. Grace always seemed at peace amongst the trees, wildflowers, and the creatures who inhabited the forest.

Grace placed her offerings in her pocket, not taking any chances, even if she told herself she wasn't sure she believed the myths.

She danced across the field and into the woods, where she felt at home. Grace sensed a swelling of joy. Hearing a greeting, she waved to the squirrel, who came out on the branch to greet her, leaving a walnut at the base of the tree for her friend. She picked a wildflower to put in her hair and left a small smooth stone at the base of the flowers for the fairies. Grace found her favorite spot against the Grandfather Tree.

Its trunk was massive, gnarled, and worn, but the lines in the trunk held secrets. Sitting against the trunk was like being held by her grandfather. She closed her eyes, and her imagination immediately began playing the stories she loved and had memorized. Relaxed, she drifted into a deep reverie.

Her eyes fluttered open. Deep brown eyes framed with dark, dense lashes, she stared at the angel lights flickering through the trees. Trees so tall she believed that if she climbed them, she would be at the gates of heaven.

The dense trees provided a timeless quality to her dream spot. Within their protection, days turned into nights, and time vanished. She was lost in the beauty and peace she found here.

When the darkness came it was the welcome kind, unlike the darkness she experienced outside the forest.

The trees stood tall and strong like the guards outside the city's walls. Those guards could be frightening, but her giant tree guards were welcoming and comforting. She could let her thoughts and dreams become a reality here.

She always wondered what else was out there, beyond the places she had traveled. Based on her ancestral stories, she knew there was a world beyond that which she could see or walk to, but would she ever know more?

She was alone, yet she didn't feel alone. She had a sense of presence. An aura of warmth, love and protection. She was never afraid in her special place.

Kalpana gazed down upon her charge. Grace was a girl of many puzzle pieces; she never knew how they would fit together, but she knew that Grace would find her way and was there to support and guide her. Grace only needed to believe and listen to her heart. Once again, their journey would continue in its new form.

Kalpana looked at the dark-haired, slightly built girl and felt her emotional journey. Journeys she had already lived in different incarnations and times, and those yet to be. The girl's past was as much a part of her future as today's journey. Kalpana was Grace's spirit guide.

Her charge would always be Grace, a name that referred to peace and beauty, yet in her many journeys, she would be known by different names. Sylvie, which represented the wood spirit and nymphs; Elissa, the wanderer; Beatrix, the traveler; and Kymarie, with wisdom beyond her years and the greatness to come. Names were chosen by parents without realizing the destiny and prophecy each name held.

Each girl had her own journey and destiny, yet they shared a unique adventure and place in time.

Full of love, Grace had eyes filled with wonder and longing, yet shadows and flickers of sorrow and loneliness lingered in her soul. She had seen and experienced much in her young life; her past held many twists, turns, and adventures. Some of her past was too distant to remember, but her soul knew the path that had been taken. Her future would hold many journeys as well. Each chapter added to the map of life.

Grace was mesmerized by the sounds in the forest, the friends in the trees, and the angel rays shining through the branches. Grace felt a presence that comforted her, even if she didn't fully understand what it was or what it meant.

In the distance, she heard her father calling her name and the sound of his footsteps as he worked his way through the dense forest towards her.

She had lulled herself into a dream where stories she had heard took her to faraway magical places. She didn't want to lose the stories, so she relived them any chance she got.

She hoped to one day learn to write her thoughts and stories down the way she saw some of the elders preserve their stories.

There were very few women who were able to do so, and she found it hard to understand why.

The berries had fallen out of the basket when she drifted off into her imagination. Hurriedly scooping them up, she ran towards the footsteps, towards her future, without even knowing it.

Kalpana watched as her charge ran through the shadows of the unknown and the light, knowing the future would play out over several lifetimes. She, herself, was looking towards the future. Her presence evaporated into the flickering angel light, ready for the next chapter. She would eventually write those chapters and share in the soul growth but, for now, on to the next journey.

Chapter 15

Sandra Novak

Sandra Novak was born into a family with a history of being able to communicate with the world of spirits.

As a child, this was a commonplace experience for her, but it was not until 1981 that a startling occurrence put her on her path of service. Sandra mysteriously doubled over as she felt a severe burning pain that pierced through the left side of her body under the armpit by her ribs. She received an intuitive message that someone of great importance had been shot. She turned on the radio and an announcement said that President Reagan had just been shot.

She was guided to attend the Berkley Psychic Institute where she was trained to enhance her skills. This led to her career as an intuitive messenger for 11 years on nationwide talk radio stations, as well as her own radio show on Maui, Hawaii.

Sandra was later guided to work with the beautiful sounds of Solar Harmonic Tuning Forks and received certification to practice.

She currently teaches Level One Tuning Fork Therapy in Arizona and travels to other states to teach a two-day course.

Sandra has 33 years of experience, which includes personal and remote readings and clearings.

www.yourenergyaligned.com

To watch our video interview scan the QR Code with your smartphone or go to: https://youtu.be/XE2MY2gfqV8

Willing to Be Me

Story of BB Wilders Bewildered
By Sandra Novak

"It is only with the heart that one can see rightly;
what is essential is invisible to the eye."
~ Antoine de Saint-Exupery

Willing to Be Me

Story of BB Wilders Bewildered

By Sandra Novak

Bea, who likes to be called BB, was the last of four children living at home with her parents. They lived in Chicago, where there was so much learning with new adventures every day.

BB felt like an only child because her three older siblings had already moved out and had families of their own. Her mother's mom (grandma) lived with them for a short while.

BB was very quiet and reserved most of the time. She had a few friends she played with. She walked to school, which was only two blocks away, and enjoyed it because she loved the different seasons. The winter snow was exciting because BB liked making snow angels. She liked the quietness and gentle fall of snowflakes on her face. Summer was fun because she could be riding her bike at the park.

She lived in a neighborhood with a few homes that had businesses inside them. One of her favorites was a corner store about a block away from her home. When BB was 10 years old, the owners allowed her to buy ice cream or candy and put the amount due on a piece of paper. Then her father would go to the store once a week to pay the tab.

Her dad worked and was gone early in the morning and didn't get home until dinner. Mom took care of the house and grandma the best she could.

Mom drank occasionally, but BB didn't like being around her when she was drinking. Going outside in nature gave BB a sense of peace. It allowed her to just enjoy being a kid. The park and its surroundings were her happy place and she spent countless hours there. When the streetlights came on, it was time to go home.

The park was big and had huge oak and maple trees, swing sets, teeter totters, sandboxes, monkey bars, lots of benches and water fountains.

She loved spending summer days riding her bike through the park, admiring all the beautiful flowers and birds. Her favorite flowers were lilac, daffodils, tulips and Lily of the Valley.

The big oak trees seemed to be very protective and had a sense of peace about them. In the fall, the beautiful maple trees were bursting with colors of yellows and oranges. BB liked to sit under any tree, listening intently to see if she could hear its quiet whispers. She felt at peace and safe while sitting under her beloved trees. BB believed they had a story to tell of all the experiences they had throughout their lifetimes in this park.

When BB was a child, an annual weekend event in the autumn was when she and her dad would go mushroom hunting in the forest not too far from where they lived. They had to find a stick to rustle through the beautiful colored leaves on the ground to find the mushrooms. Each carried a basket, and, by the end of the day, it would be filled with mushrooms.

One time, BB started to wander and was so engrossed in looking for mushrooms that she didn't notice how lost she was. She had been walking for quite some time and was getting thirsty and hungry. It was then that she realized she didn't know where she was, but she wasn't frightened.

As she kept walking, she looked down and came across little houses made from the bark of big oak trees, and the rooftops were like shingles of beautiful colors from the autumn leaves.

The houses were little, about 12 inches by 12 inches, and some were actually smaller. As she looked ahead, she saw lots of them. She wondered who had placed them there. As she looked up, she felt a cool breeze and the smell of delicious pine trees. The wind rustled through the pine trees, making a delicate ocean sound.

She suddenly got the feeling that she should build a tiny house, too. She thought they could be houses for fairies. Out of the corner of her eye, she saw movement and noticed what looked like Tinkerbell. So, fairies are real! Then more and more revealed themselves.

This was an important moment for BB. It finally demonstrated that what she had been seeing throughout her childhood really existed — things that her mom had said people don't talk about.

BB started to communicate with the fairies and saw that their wings looked like opals and rainbows. BB talked with her voice but heard them speak in her head. It was a quiet knowingness...

The fairies told her that they help the forest and the environment to bring in good energy to the animals, plants and trees that exist in the forest, plus light energy to the beings not always seen by human eyes.

The fairies said there was a whole network of beings who help the forest by cleaning the air and doing so much more. They also said they were thankful for all the little houses.

The fairies told BB that they assist humans in many ways. If someone is sad, all they need to do is ask for help and the fairies will assist them in raising their frequency vibration. You can visualize placing several small fairies on your shoulder. Then visualize giving one of them to people who have a lot of problems or who are sad or who might be going through a hard time. Place the fairy on their shoulder to bring more laughter, lightness and joy. Children see fairies much more than adults. As a child, BB saw fairies a lot and simply thought it was the way things were. She didn't realize until adulthood that most other people didn't see fairies like she could.

The wind was growing stronger, and BB was getting tired and cold. She said her goodbyes and told the fairies that she would be back again. She called out for her father and felt a little feeling of panic when she realized that she really was lost. Little did she know that her father had been following behind her all that time. A feeling of relief came over her when she saw him. BB asked her father if he could see the little fairies. He just had a big smile and winked.

As a young girl BB would see colors around people. Some were bright and pretty, while others were dark and icky looking.

When someone passed away in the family, BB didn't understand why people were crying standing by the casket. That's because BB could see the person who passed away hovering above their own body or standing next to it and smiling. When BB told her mother about what she saw, she was told, "You can't say that. It's your imagination. Shhh…No more talk like that."

As BB was growing into an adult, she had many strange experiences that seemed to have no answers. One day in her twenties, she was standing in the foyer of her home and felt a bullet enter the left side of her body below the armpit near the rib cage. In her head, she heard a message that said someone of great importance had just been shot.

The first person she thought of was her mother who lived a few miles away. BB got her two children into the car and started driving to her mother's house. On the way, she turned on the radio to hear the announcement that President Reagan had just been shot.

Questions started flooding her mind like, "Why me? Why did I get this message? What am I supposed to do with this information?" In the coming year, BB would learn why the gift of intuition was going to be her greatest gift allowing her to be of service to others.

When she felt it was time to move to a warmer climate, she was amazed at how the universe provides answers for us if we simply tune in, listen and follow our intuition. BB did move and started a new life with her children.

If you have any feelings that don't feel quite right but they're getting your attention, trust your intuition. It's always spot on and has your highest and best interests at heart.

And, who knows? You just might start a conversation with the fairies!

Chapter 16

Sara Newman

My name is Sara Newman, also known as Glowla, the LA Tooth Fairy.

I grew up in the Berkshires of Western, MA., where as a child, I made friends with the flower fairies in our beautiful English garden. I believed they were real, and to this day, I still do.

WHY create The LA Tooth Fairy? As an actor, I have experience in Children's Theater and have always loved entertaining kids. In our fast-paced world, kids grow up so quickly. I want to be someone who helps preserve the magic of childhood, just a little longer.

We know the story of Santa Claus, but little is known about the Tooth Fairy. I wrote Glowla's story in hopes that she will be woven into our mythology with an environmental message. Playing Glowla brings me the utmost joy. I look forward to bringing that same delight to you and your family!

Tooth Fairy Glowla can be found spreading fairy joy, doing live performances in person (currently in Los Angeles), and over Zoom for children all over the world. If you know a little one who would love a tooth fairy encounter, visit LAtoothfairy.com

And follow on IG: l.a.toothfairy. Her fairy door is always open to those who seek it.

The Tale of Glowla The Tooth Fairy

A Story for Children
By Sara Newman

Everything that is real was imagined first.
~The Velveteen Rabbit

The Tale of Glowla
The Tooth Fairy

A Story for Children

By Sara Newman

This is the real story of a real fairy making mischief and magic in all the corners of the world.

Glowla was born at the stroke of midnight when most magical things take place. Her bright glow inspired her mother to name her just so. From the time of their birth, a fairy can live for a thousand years! This twinkling story begins on Glowla's 200th birthday.

Once upon a time, before big cities existed, nature and magic were where fairies dwelled. At that time, Glowla was an ordinary fairy, a little shy, a little quiet, with a big knack for adventure. She adored making silly mischief with her best friends, Flash and Aquaria. They excelled in doing what most fairies do best. They protected the land by planting trees or guiding the bees to find their perfect flower. Fairies put dew drops on the grass, cleaned the water and the air, while others simply basked in the sun. Those sun fairies really knew how to relax; you can usually find them in Southern California.

When the fairies weren't mischief-making, sunbathing, or tinkering in the natural world, they loved to make their fairy homes beautiful. Creating a cozy home brings pride and joy. One of the kindest things a human can do is to craft a fairy house. Have YOU ever built a fairy house? Fairies make special houses inside tree trunks, and could live happily there, for a long time. Until one day... something happened, and it changed everything.

PEOPLE! People came and began cutting down their tree homes to build large houses, tall buildings, and highways. Eventually, the land that flourished turned into bustling cities. The fairies tried to plant trees, and bushes to hide in, but everything kept being chopped, cut, and destroyed. The old, magical fairy world was being forgotten and left behind.

Glowla never forgot the night her fairy tree was cut. Fast asleep in her little leaf bed, nestled on her flower petal pillow; suddenly, she felt herself falling down, down, down! Crashing right to the ground, she bumped her head, then fell into a deep sleep where she was visited by hear Great, Great Grandfather Bristlecone Fairy. He had a big mustache and a long beard. "Glowla!" cried Bristlecone. "The fairies are in grave danger! You must save our kind from doom and gloom! Find the invincible seed that will save the fairies.

Since Glowla had never heard the word invisible, she asked Bristlecone what that meant. In his deep, wisdom-resounding voice, he answered, "It is something that cannot be destroyed." He continued, "Plant the invincible seed with the root as it will grow an invincible tree and the fairies will have tree homes once again. Remember, find the seed with a root for the invincible tree! Stay alert! Keep your eyes open! You will find it in an unlikely place!" Then his long beard began turning into swirly dust, and he vanished!

Glowla awoke to the sound of the whispering wind, which is how fairies communicate, like text messaging through the air. The winds whispered, "Glowla. Wake up! It's time for the fairy council meeting in the secret special spot, at the stroke of midnight, which is right now!! Go, fly Glowla!!"

Arriving, she joined hundreds of her fairy tribe under the big oak tree with the twinkling firefly-like lights. The fairies were in a frenzy, babbling all at once!

"What do we do?"

"We must all leave!"

"But this is our home! We've been here for all of time!"

"But if we stay we'll get squashed!

"Yeah, I keep flying into an evil invisible thing the people call "windows." Ouch, ouch ouch! They all agreed. Nobody liked windows.

The Fairies deliberated all night, into the next day, until the sun rose and fell thirty times.

Then, Flash, who was late to the meeting, came flying in, shouting as loud as a fairy possibly can, "I have News! I've just been to the Good Witch of the ocean. She's made a potion that makes a fairy grow to the size of a human being. Any fairy brave enough to drink it can stay here, blend in with the people, and will no longer get squashed. Look, See?

He pulled out a potion. It shimmered green, twas an unusual alga from the ocean.

Who will take the potion? Who will do it? Nobody was coming forward.

Then, something inside of Glowla began bubbling up, like a firefly rising from the grass at dusk. And she REMEMBERED HER DREAM! "I'll do it," Glowla said as loud as she could!

Everyone gasped! "Oh! Ohh! OHH!" Yet, she knew this was her chance.

"I had a dream that Great Great Grandfather Bristlecone told me to find the invincible seed with a root. So if I find this special, indestructible seed, then it will grow into an indestructible tree. Should I find lots of these seeds, I can grow enough tree homes for everyone! Besides, humans need trees to breathe, and fairies to believe in —especially children. They are losing their belief in magic, but we can bring it back"!

"But how, how HOW?" asked the fairies.

"I don't know, I simply have to try!" said Glowla. Quickly, before she could change her mind, Glowla grabbed the magical potion. In that very moment, she became brave, and would never be the same again. She took a big drink. "GULP"

At first, nothing, and then… Her big toe began to grow! "Oh, oh, Oh, that's a very big toe," said the fairies. Then in her feet, she felt some heat! Next, her legs shot like big beanstalks; and her middle began to wiggle. Glowla's belly button grew so big, she stuck her tiny head inside and let out a shout that echoed as if in a cave.

Helloooooo in therrrrrre!!!!!!!!!!!!!!

Her arms shot out like a chameleon's tongue. Her hair sprouted like fresh spaghetti one by one! She felt her wings, look at these things! And then her face took up more space!

Glowla spotted a nearby pond and flew over to see her reflection. There she was! BIG BIG BIG! Apparently, if you eat your greens, you really do grow! It's amazing! She was ready to take on her quest! But where to begin?

The fairies stood in awe as she towered above them. "But what about her wings?" Someone said. She does NOT look human!

Everyone turned to Bookie the Bard fairy. who was terribly smart and read human books all day. Bookie was an expert on Human things.

Bookie spoke: "Well... Humans do this thing where they dress up and pretend to be something else for fun. It's called Halloweenie.

"Haaaalloweeeenie" they said aloud. They all liked the sound of that!

"Theoretically," said Bookie, "Glowla can pretend to be human pretending to be a fairy. She can say she's doing Halloweenie, and nobody will question it! Once again, everyone began blabbing all at once, making a whole lot of fairy hubbub.

"Hey what a good idea, this might actually work," said the fairies to each other.

Flash and Aquaria helped Glowla prepare for her departure. She tucked all of her fairy clothes in a bag, and suddenly felt sad. Her favorite fairy outfits, the ones of flowers and bark and moss, no longer fit.

"There is one thing I forgot to mention," said Flash. "The potion wears off. After a few hours, you'll go back to being tiny again.

No sooner did Flash say it, she shrunk down, down, down, down, down into her normal fairy size! "Ahhh, I'm myself again," thought Glowla. "Halloweenie will be fun, but I don't want to do it *all* the time," she mused.

And so began Glowla's search for an invincible seed. She flew to the city of Los Angeles first, because they only had palm trees and she figured they could use some variety! She planted everything she could find. She found apple cores in garbage cans and planted an orchard. She found watermelon seeds in the sand at the beach. She planted a whole patch, but before she knew it, someone turned it into a parking garage. That was odd, she didn't plant parking garage seeds!

Her pine trees were cleared out for a studio lot. She'd plant and plant, and they'd destroy and destroy. Finding an invincible seed was starting to feel impossible.

"I can't give up" she told herself, even when things felt hard.

Since her search took almost one-hundred years, it is a good thing fairies live a long time! Then one day, as Glowla was daydreaming in a park, a young child stopped along her path, pulled out a very wiggly tooth, looked at it curiously for a moment, and then tossed it on the ground right where Glowla was perched.

Out of habit really, she picked it up and planted it. Then the most miraculous thing happened, it began to grow, and grow and grow and grow! Glowla remembered what Bristlecone had said, "Plant a seed with a root," Well, a tooth has a root! and from a human Child's mouth was certainly an "unlikely place" just like the Great Grandfather said it would be.

Testing its invincibility, Glowla tried to knock it, wack it, cut it, crack it, but the little tooth tree would not budge. Glowla sent a whisper in the wind to find Flash and Aquaria to spread the news to the other fairies. Pretty soon, all of the fairies were writing letters to the children and asking them to put their teeth under the pillow for the fairies to find.

With the help of children, together they could live in harmony with humans, keeping their magic close by.

The tooth trees were just the beginning of the magical powers that baby teeth held when in the hands of a fairy. For inside a baby tooth, is a child's essence.

It's the childlike wonder that fairies share with children which is curiosity, play, mischief, innocence, joy, and pureness of heart. Glowla now asks that the children, upon the loss of a baby tooth, please place it under their pillow for her to find. And in return, she'll gift something to keep as a memory.

As you grow up, try to hold onto your inner child, for there is magic there, that is the same likeness, as the magic of fairies. Remember, Glowla can only use healthy teeth, don't forget to brush AND floss. Pinky swear?

Oh, and if you also want to leave her a midnight snack, she loves Honey Nut Cheerios!

Chapter 17

Sharyn G. Jordan-McWhorter

Sharyn G. Jordan-McWhorter
Anthologist, Storyteller, Home Whisperer

Dedicated to BEing an enthusiastic JOY-Bringer, Sharyn is a Story Alchemist, a Smith of the Word, and a Feng Shui Master. Through her environmental healing expertise and lifetime as a writer, she lovingly and wisely guides her clients/students along the Tao of Exquisite Living.

Sharyn, known internationally as the Home Whisperer since 1994, merges practical magic, mystery, and mythical secrets into her Feng Shui Simplified Consultancy. Her ancient yet evolved, modern-day system results in discovering one's inner Muse and outer Miracles. Indeed, Home is our Memoir.

From 1970 - 1972, in Mazatlán, Mexico, she was a student in the spiritual study of the timeless I-Ching. She incorporated this wisdom into her consultation. Since 1975, she has taught the BE-Jeweled Treasure Mapping process, which made her a multi-millionaire.

In 2013, Sharyn founded the Wind-Water Conservatory, whose curriculum includes WISDOM: the Way of the Writerly. its nine-month online classroom midwives. inspires and informs birthing her writerly students' projects, passion, and purposes. Plus, their chapter babies are included in her current year's anthology. Her three Guiding Grace Volumes I, II, and III are oracles, an abiding source of encouragement, and are testaments to the gratitude, growth, and goodness of the Human Spirit.

Having owned and operated eight businesses, some bricks and mortar, such as five Arizona movie theatres in Lakeside, Pinetop, Show Low, Winslow, and Holbrook; Rosebud Preschool, and Seven Streams of Energy, she understands the value of leadership, serving from the heart, vision, tenacity, and perseverance.

Her service-oriented enterprises are as follows:

1. Feng Shui Simplified Consultancy of Transformation
2. One-OM-One Nine Star Chi Insights
3. Creating Sacred Space based on the Five Elements, Bagua, and I-Ching
4. BE-Jeweled Treasure Mapping Excellence
5. Wind-Water Conservatory: elevating, expanding, and enriching her student's personal journey through the Power of Story.
6. Triangulus 3 Publishing, LLC: Anthologist
7. Enagic: Magic/Energy; Water Wellness Technology

In her "Fairytales Do Come True" Chapter, Sharyn tells how she wrote herself into the greatest love story of her life with her Gem. With a deep dedication to family and the blessings of having written historical fiction novels, political thrillers, and biographies (to date, there are nine books), she is in awe, in divine gratitude. and is extremely honored to BE Living the incredible Life she Loves.

Sharyn can BE Reached via:
Classroom@fengshuisimplifed.com

For further information and to receive a muse-worthy word, Visit her website, FengShuiSimplified.com

To view our interview with Sharyn, please scan the QR Code with your smartphone or go to:
https://youtu.be/uc4uFwZY46Q

Fairytales Do Come True

By Sharyn G. Jordan-McWhorter

"Writing of our greatest ecstasies is divine, Penning the life we love is forever sublime, The universe always proves our musings, 'write?' Let us scribe beauty, bliss, blessings & of joy's delight."

~Sharyn G. Jordan-McWhorter
Anthologist. Storyteller, & Home Whisperer

Fairytales Do Come True

By Sharyn G. Jordan-McWhorter

*H*ave you ever seen the 1984 classic film *Romancing The Stone?* Its ingenious plot finds the leading role, Joan, radiantly played by Kathleen Turner, as a successful romance writer who, in real life, has nary a love interest. She was too involved in her work to even stock the fridge or have tissues nearby to cry into after completing her novel. The reclusive world she created was safe until, en route to her editor, a mysterious man pressed a treasure map into her hand. Upon inspection, it revealed the location of an exquisite emerald stone that had been secretly ensconced in Columbia. Suddenly, she is whisked into a spectacular adventure and becomes the daring character she had written about for years. Did I mention Michael Douglas was also in the movie? Indeed, it is a quest of the heart.

With my lifelong love of fairytales, fables, and folklore going back as far as I can recall, this movie was my CUPPA. Growing up, every night, my dear father enthralled my younger sister, sweet Suzanne, and me with stories by Hans Christian Anderson, olden tales compiled by the Brothers Grimm, plus Zane Grey and Perry Mason novels. We learned the value of courage, never giving up, and the supremacy of love. Since Dad encouraged us to craft our storied missions, when I was eleven, my sister and I began writing a captivating fairytale series set in the enchanted Dragon Woods. Our protagonist was Magda Rose, an ethereal ghost whom I "met" during our summer vacations in the majestic New Mexico forest.

This fostered a deep love of writing, reading, experiencing as many as three movies a week, and enjoying musicals such as *South Pacific, The King and I, Oklahoma,* and *West Side Story* enriched my enthusiasm for make-believe. I never identified with the Shero; I preferred writing the stories.

Magical opportunities continuously opened my heart. It piqued my curiosity and found me in awe when, in 1969, I met my late husband in a fairy tale setting. On a starlit night, I stood in the local park's heavenly-scented rose garden while attending a Memorial Day music festival. I was mesmerized by the song being sung; it was "Some Enchanted Evening." Oh, yes, from the musical South Pacific. Looking through the garden's beauty, I saw a beautiful boy my age walking towards me; when our eyes met, it was love at first sight. Unexpectedly, several mates scooped him up to sing with the band. I had to leave and for the remainder of the summer, this magical song played everywhere I went, even at the dentist's. Truly, it was the promise of our finding one another again.

Three months later, in synchronicity, I was formally introduced to my beloved Jay, the beautiful boy from the park at my cousin Buz's Texas Barbecue. Our whirlwind romance swept us off our feet, and in just another three months, we were majestically, magically married. For forty-two years, we were blessed with an adventurously magnificent life of loving and far too many miracles to list. Our precious children and grands, owning movie theatres, and traveling extensively, were all dreams that came true. Being together all of those years was divine. Jay's 2012 transition was devastating.

Traversing the bridge of sorrow to joy, I was blessed to focus on teaching the spiritual blessings of Treasure Mapping that I learned in 1975, now widely known as vision boarding. Indeed, real-life, fantastical fairy tales unfolded for my excellent students. I also tapped into and continued aligning with my intention of dwelling in beauty, joy, and divine gratitude. In addition, my Home Whisperer expertise was especially healing. Since 1994, I have been honored to create sacred sanctuaries for my beloved clients. In 2007, my Feng Shui Simplified - Treasures of the Inner and Outer Home book was published. Indeed, my heart overflowed with such appreciation. Feeling incredibly esteemed, I was 'write' where I was supposed to BE.

Indeed, the universe always proves our musings. In the early summer of 2022, I was still basking in the glow of our 2021 compilation Guiding Grace Series, Volume I, *Wisdom of the Silver Sisters,* a best-seller. I was immersed in Volume II's *Golden Wisdom of Love, Legend, and Legacies* project when my father, who passed away in 1962, came to me in a celestial dream. He was with hundreds of our ancestors, sending me their blessings and vivid images of our 1959 fairytale. My dearest father's mythical message was, "You are embarking on a "Mission Possible," to rewrite our sublime story, teaching humanity how to create a pristine future."

Through my Wind-Water Conservatory Wisdom: The Writerly Way, Magda grew into Willow Rose. Thus, my Ava-STARR of Dragon Wood, an Apothecary, Alchemist, and Artist, was Nostradamus's goddaughter and amazingly advanced into the historical fiction genre. The exhilaration I experienced researching her era of medieval France was riveting. Born in 1540, Willow lived during the rapturous Renaissance. It was also during the horrific religious wars. The entire book process enriched my fertile imagination, refueled my reservoirs of resources, and helped me better understand history. It was awe-inspiring. Authoring a fairy tale of such magnitude drew me into a realm of enchantment where anything is possible.

While deep-diving into universal patterns, humanitarian issues, and spiritual growth themes, best of all, Willow found true love. Her beloved husband, Etienne, came into her sacred world.

Since Willow has been to the future, she knows what this precious life requires. Her beguiling albeit bold quests reveal long-held mysteries; she catalyzes change. As an Apothecary and a healer, Willow posed a significant threat to the religious world. With a bounty on her head, she was forced to go underground into her family's catacombs below the streets of Lyon, France. At risk, she may never see her beloved Etienne or their children again. Just as she faithfully did over their years together, when they were physically apart, she wrote love letters to her beloved Etienne.

My Beloved Etienne,

Before time began, the mesmeric winds were singing our names. Calling us to waft within the wild rivers weave. In 1555 A.D., we were wed, intimately intertwined. Soaring over the ancient rose gardens that bloom our eternal love and into our cherished Enchanted Woods, we are as one. I am holding your heart to mine, forever and a day. I cannot shake an eerie foreboding that if this is perhaps my last love letter to you, as always, it was written from my soul to yours. My beloved, know you abide in the deepest part of my devoted being. Traversing time and space, bringing all around me from the essence of our never-ending incarnation to reincarnation, life after life, is the story of our luminous love. Finding one another once again in this life is transcendent. You are my inspiration. Together, we constellate through the Milky Way and beyond the galaxies of this world.

Eagerly, I await your safe return. I feel you right beside me, musing over you. 'Tis just as brilliant as it was when our eyes first met. In the magical summer of 1555, en route on the Camino Santiago, seeing you with your black curls cascading in wild abandon, emerald-green eyes, and a bright smile lit up the universe, you pierced my heart with love. My fifteen-year-old self knew you, a boy-man, a mere nineteen years of age, was my eternal Soulmate. From our life of blessings to blessings, upon my heart is deep gratitude, my dearest Etienne.

…To be continued.

Steeped in the charms of this fantastic world, little did I know my life was about to go inside out, upside down, and become far better and beyond what I dreamed. You see, after my husband passed away, I leaned into gratitude and gave myself the gifts of both grace and grief. As an homage to my 'old' life, I gently traversed the mercies of loss and healing. Building a bridge from sorrow to joy was a tendered mercy, such an elegant process.

Creating a life of "We" into "Me" was a process. I was grateful for my cherished family, amazing friends, a rewarding consulting and coaching career, and the deep fulfillment of being a published writer. For ten years, eight months, and ten days of being a widow revealed inner strength, refined gifts of service, and refueled the sacred belief in the triple treasure of divine will, wisdom, and wonderment.

Miraculously, the tides turned, revealing the promised land of milk and honey. Right out of a Happily-Ever-After story, James, a widower and trusted family friend since 1982, and I unexpectedly began to fall in love. We discovered that beyond enjoying the same books and movies, we relished dining, laughing, long walks, and waxing philosophically; we most loved being together. Since he is a rare treasure who tenderly holds my heart affectionately, I call him my Gem. In 2022, we became a couple by never pushing the river, being in the flow, and dwelling in beauty, gratitude, and joy. Our true-to-life extraordinary story continues to bless us.

In the golden hour of a bejeweled autumn Sunday on October 15, 2023, we were over the moon in Moon Valley, Arizona, to become husband and wife. Our mutual exuberance for one another fills our hearts with joy and uplifts our spirits; every day is a honeymoon. We dwell at the intersection of beauty and blessings. Writing ourselves into our greatest ecstasies and, by far, discovering we are the supreme love of our lives is divine. Indeed, I am Willow Rose to my Gem's Etienne. In this life, we found one another once again.

Fairytales Do Come True.

Chapter 18

Susan M. Botich

Storyteller, Poet, Songwriter, and Musician

Throughout her twenties, Ms. Botich worked as a professional musician, playing her original story-songs, along with established music. She met and married the love of her life, shifting her focus on having a family. While devoting her attention to motherhood and marriage, she felt the time right to shift her creative endeavors to poetry and story writing. During that time, she would write during "the wee hours" – that magical time between midnight and early morning.

Since an early age, she had been fascinated with stories rich in myth and metaphor. From classic mythological tales to traditional and contemporary folk tales, their rich symbolism and allegory kept her reading into the late hours and pondering their universal truths.

The myth of a righteous ruler who brings peace to all mankind through reigning with compassion and justice is not confined to one culture alone. But the story of King Arthur, and the unity he created at a time when the world more than ever needed peace, particularly won her heart. Enchantments was born out of that love.

Also published by Susan M. Botich:
The Dream Star.

For more information, visit:
https://www.facebook.com/SusanMBotichBooks

To view our video interview with Susan, please scan the QR Code with your smartphone, or go to:
https://youtu.be/j88-rSmQlcc

"Follow your bliss."
—Joseph Campbell

ENCHANTMENTS is an allegorical tale based on Arthurian myth, told in prose and verse.

Though born and raised in the elven land of E'alowen, E'lienna, daughter of Lady Claire, a human, and Gle'anden, prince of elves, longs to better understand her human lineage. She sets out from E'alowen and into human lands. There, she visits the wizened Mage of Dur, a long-time friend to her parents and all elvenkind. She discovers that the wizard is secretly working to help bring about a new age throughout the land of humankind. For he reveals to her that a babe, born of a king, has been secretly hidden away until such time when he is grown so that he may fulfill a prophesy made long ago of a king of men who will grow to rule the land with justice and mercy.

Through her quest to find out more about her mother's mysterious past and about this righteous king of men, E'lienna uncovers the mystery behind a tragedy that befell her family years ago and, in the process, discovers that the worlds of men and elves are much more deeply entwined than either believed.

Enchantments

By Susan M. Botich

My name is E'lienna. I am daughter to a human woman and an elven prince. It is this very thing that brings up longing deep within me to find my own place in both worlds.

Many stories tell of how the worlds of men and elves are weaving. This is my own story. So listen, if you've mind to hear, and I'll recount my tale to you in that fashion keeping with the long-held elf tradition: poetry and prose entwining.

THE BEGINNING

While moon shines bright and full, I ride out from my elven wood, E'alowen, and under hood and cloak, I keep myself quite hidden...

THE UNICORN

Deep in the wood,
where stillness seems to have a soul
and evening's sky is a dark blue bowl,
whether it was wise or good,
Claire went searching for the glade—
the glade where last the tracks were found
by the man from Brackentown.

THE IMAGINIST

Bathed in moonlight,
the open grassy meadow shimmered.
A rippling pond, like diamonds, glimmered.
She chose a spot, concealed by night,
and there she sat and there she stayed
and hid behind the swaying shadows
of a tree's low boughs.

Her eyes grew tired
while breezy rhythms soothed and lulled.
She fought the sleep that tugged and pulled,
and pondered on what had inspired
that strange, old man, bent and grayed,
reflecting on the tale she'd heard,
muttered from his tangled beard.

At last she heard
the distant rhythm of the beating—
hooves shaking earth with every meeting!
She froze there, silent—not a word.
With all her mind, she hoped and prayed
that she could steal, before the morn,
one glance of his silvery horn.

The beating grew,
yet, with each pounding step, her heart
felt surely it might burst apart.
'Twas not 'til then, she truly knew
the terrible mistake she'd made.
For, "Only those of purest spirit
may venture to go near it."

She listened, spellbound,
to the beating of those ancient hooves, like
hail upon a hundred roofs!
Then, suddenly, there came no sound. Only
breezes softly played.

184

ENCHANTMENTS

She wondered to herself, amazed,
in the midnight, damp and hazed.

She would have run.
But something kept her rooted there—
A force I can't describe or share.
She knew that nothing could be done.
So, 'til the night began to fade
and, quiet, close its thousand eyes,
she sang soft lullabies.

Time ceased to spin.
She sang and sang of childhood dreams,
where hope still shines, and trust still gleams.
Her songs swelled up from deep within.
So long had she been there, delayed,
the gold sun rose and warmed her through
while she sat amid the dew.

Finally still,
her songs had spun their last sweet stories of
noble creatures and noble glories.
The meadow glowed like dream—so tranquil.
The dew, emeralds on every blade.
She marveled at such simple beauty—
a miracle to see.

In that silence,
It then felt right to take her leave,
She hadn't seen him yet couldn't grieve.
Her life had, thus, been just—events,
while that night had been a trade
of fancies for true miracles.
Not magic animals.

'Twas then he came.
Not thundering with frightening speed,

but gently walked the mythic steed.
And as he neared, he spoke her *name*
then knelt before her as if bade,
bowing down his spiraled horn.
The ancient unicorn!

THE ELVES

From the time Claire was a little girl,
she'd heard the stories of the elves.
Yet, more than merely tales they'd seemed,
held inside old books that waited
lonely on the shelves,
more than just some notion dreamed,
more than simple bedtime stories
of good men and their glories.

She'd loved those stories of the elves!
—How they'd help a stranger, lost;
heal his wounds, feed his soul
and share their stories, in sweet songs,
of courage and the cost,
and what it is that makes us whole,
and how it is they'd come to cherish
that which will not perish.

She dreamed of traveling far from home to
find some ancient, magic wood where she
would meet one for herself. She'd bring a
single, precious gift
and give it, if she could,
to one tall, slender, gentle elf.
The gift—her treasured crystal locket,
kept safe in her pocket.

ENCHANTMENTS

A locket made by ancient hands
which, opened, would reveal some truth.
Then she would play some simple part
in helping good souls find their way,
and wise, in spite of youth,
she'd help return them to the heart,
where all true victories are won
and evil deeds undone.

Well, years passed by, and Claire grew up.
Forgetting magic woods and elves
and busy with her daily cares,
she spent her time in hopeless toil
with those who served themselves.
Trapped within life's cunning snares—
that shadowed world of half-truth lies;
deceits clouded her eyes.

And thus she spent each sadder day.
Having lost her dreams of heart,
she filled her life with work and things
of comfort and of costly beauty,
further set apart
from magic and its lucent wings.
She'd lost her life. Yet, fearing death,
she grieved with every breath.

Until one evening full of stars,
during summer's hot embrace,
for no reason that she could recall,
she chose to take a walk along
a lonely, wooded place.
From there inside, she heard a call
so strange and song like in its tone
It thrilled her to her bone!

She thought of crazy wanderers.
She thought of cruel men and of thieves.
But still, from somewhere deep within,
she knew these voices held no threat.
(The child within believes!)
'Twas then she heard the call again.
From far within the trees she heard
one solitary word.

"Come," the voices sang to her.
"Come," they sang so high and sweet.
'Twas then old memories flooded in
and spilled out from her weary eyes
and fell about her feet.
She wept and sobbed and wept and then,
with all those memories full and swollen,
knew what had been stolen.

She ran into the wood so fast
her feet flew, barely touching ground!
Frantically she searched the place
from where the tender voices sang
but no one could be found.
"Why tease then vanish with no trace?"
she cried, and dropped down to her knees
and wept among the trees.

She saw her life so clearly, then.
She knew the truth and knew the lies.
And that was when she made her choice
to walk away and not look back,
no matter what the ties.
'Twas on that day, Claire found her voice.
She stood up straight and stood up tall
and softly sang her call.

ENCHANTMENTS

"Come," she whispered like a sigh.
Again she sang it, "Come to me."
With all her heart and all her mind,
she focused on her childhood spirit
still alive in memory.
And with such faith (that some call blind),
she kept repeating, "Come. Come!
Come and take me home!"

Finally wind began to stir
and all the leaves began to dance.
She breathed in deeply summer's scent,
sweet and pungent on her tongue
and, nourished by its fragrance,
once again she sang her chant.
"I will not leave until you come!
Come and take me home!"

She sensed them first, before she saw.
(The leaves were rustling like a sigh.)
She did not move but for her breath.
While light and shadow wildly played,
a star fell from the sky.
She watched its brief pass into death
and when she turned from that black bowl,
their gazes pierced her soul!

She knew them all, though not by name.
Yet, so familiar was each face
that each one seemed a long-lost friend.
And warm affection filled her breast
when they, with royal grace,
bowed low, their arms outstretched, palms opened,
waiting there in silent night
while bathed in full moon light.

Then the tallest of them smiled
and gave his hand for Claire to take.
"I am Gle'anden. We have come
from far away E'alowen,
across the Crystal Lake.

We've come, at last, to take you home.
For though your mind became deceived,
your heart always believed!"

Now while Gle'anden spoke these words,
the other elves all circled 'round.
And all the forest was transformed
to dancing light, like silver threads,
from topmost bough to ground.
Claire just smiled, quiet, warmed.
It all was good, it all was right—
this symphony of light.

Then, swept up in that symphony, they
danced and sang themselves—away.
Until the wood was just a wood
and silent as the dark itself.
Yet, on the ground, there lay
one silver thread where last they'd stood,
shimmering in the soft moonlight.
A memory of the night.

Now, there's a land that's far away, where
forests sprawl out lush and green and
lakes and rivers dance and shine and fill
the sky with rainbow hues,
the loveliest you've seen!
There, the folks are good and fine. Claire
lives there, with Gle'anden, in E'alowen.

ENCHANTMENTS

Chapter 19

Suzanne Anderson

Suzanne Anderson was born in 1928 and says she is now getting younger and is changing time and space.

Always an educator, she was certified in three levels in Montessori Education: hands-on methods for preschool, kindergarten, and elementary education. She was the director of her school in Bozeman, MT. She won an award for writing curriculum with American Montessori for her master's project on the Mineral Kingdom.

Her first love is Sacred Geometry. She has studied with the acclaimed British Master Teacher Keith Critchlow at the KAIROS Foundation. The fairytale that appears in this book titled ***Codes and Toads,*** delves into this profound world. Due to blindness, in order to bring her incredible story to the printed page, she dictated it from memory. It was then transcribed. Suzanne is a natural storyteller. We look forward to the future adventures of her Ava-STARRS, preteen twins Caron and Baron, plus their Uncle Homer Wentworth.

Suzanne is a perpetual student who explores the mysteries of the universe and teaches its myths, miracles, and magic. She is the esteemed matriarch of seven children and hopes to inspire her twenty-five grandchildren and more than thirty-five great grandchildren.

Codes and Toads

By Suzanne Anderson

"Stories are seed syllables that grow,
make up, and create words."
~Suzanne Anderson

Codes and Toads

by Suzanne Anderson

Caron and Baron, pre-teen twins, were thrilled to enjoy their summer vacation in France at their Uncle Homer Wentworthy's majestic estate. To be away from their regular, demanding academic schedule was blissful. Knowing they would have unusual adventures, even though Uncle was a weird character and a little hard to get along with because he's very elderly and is not fond of children, they were still happy.

However, after five days of gloomy rain, they were completely bored. It was almost too much to expect the children to endure being shut in. Plus, their crotchety old uncle's ill health and chronic negativity were beginning to wear on them. They wanted to explore the grounds, create, and go on quests. With the wind being particularly blustery, they thought how fun it would be to fly their kites if only the rain would cease. Amazingly, the rain stopped at the very same time when this thought occurred to them.

Without hesitation, with kites in hand, they bolted, ran outside, and were ecstatic to embark on a flying frolic. Immediately, the kites soared up and away, and then Caron's kite crashed far into the treetops. Being the brave-hearted one, always leaping before she looked, she thought nothing of going into the woods to retrieve her kite. Baron, by nature, is a rule follower, and this challenge raised multiple red flags. Rather reluctant, if even a little bit frightened, to venture into the foreboding forest, Baron is a formidable naysayer of most adventures. Caron pushes him forward; he pulls back. His retiring emeritus and her bold poise usually take them in different directions, only to end up on the same side of the task.

Caron is already skipping along into the woods, not bothering to obey what she sees as unwritten rules. Assured of their success, she promises her brother it is safe. After all, how spooky can it be? She trusts the process. Imagining where the kite could have landed, Caron is oblivious to the creatures in the forest. When Baron calls after her, she hears anxiety in his voice and doubles back. She sees he has come across an old toad that captures their interest. They had heard if you pick them up, you may pick up warts, too.

They decide to catch the toad, yet he keeps hopping away, staying just out of their reach. Could this be the beginning of a quest? Their last adventure was with the Hopi Indians in the American Southwest. During one of the tribe's native Kachina dancers' ceremonies, Caron connected with the iconic performer, a legendary warrior.

Each of the toad's leaps led them deeper into the forest. While chasing it, they bumped headlong into the very tree in which Caron's kite had crashed. At that point, the twins decided to climb up and rescue it. Caron scaled up one side and Baron, the other, then CRACK, Caron's limb gave way. Down she went, landing on a soft mound of dirt on a hillside. It immediately collapsed, swallowing her up.

Baron finds the courage to jump in after her. They found themselves in a mysterious cave. All they could see from the ground was a ceiling made of sparkling crystals. With the impact of their sudden drop, crystal dust sprinkled them from head to toe.

They both sighed, grateful to be intact. This experience left them more curious than fearful. Shaking off the sparkling dust, they looked around. There was the same ugly toad looking back at them. The walls appear to be covered in symbols of spirals, triangles, circles, diamonds, and arches. Immediately, their adventurous souls recognized this was another step in their quest.

Just past the inscribed wall was a much larger space, a sanctuary. A beam of light streamed in from the tall ceiling, illuminating a statue resembling the Warrior Kachina they once met.

Taller than a human, he was poised on one foot, with the other one raised, and standing on a large sphere the size of a beach ball. He has four arms, two on each side, and the number eight sideways on his navel. His face is covered with a cloth revealing only the features of a nose and a mouth; the cloth has two slits for eyes with tasseled corners. The stature seemed to be made of a strange metal, while his body build resembled an Atlas. The children knew Atlas wasn't shrugging because the dancing Kachina was perfectly poised.

On his head is a 7-level tower resembling the layers of a wedding cake. His hands were holding geometric solids. The form of a pyramid was in one hand, a diamond form on another, and on the other hand, was a multi-triangular faceted form. In the fourth hand was an object that resembled a miniature soccer ball made out of twenty pentagrams.

Knowing there are further mysteries to be solved, they are even more invested. What is Dancing Kachina's message? Getting closer to the statue, Caron and Baron saw words carved in the ledge around the bottom of the sphere. "To be forever young, drink here!" And, on the back side, "Drink here to be forever young." It works both ways.

To solve this mystery may mean they should ask Uncle Homer for help. They both knew it was time to look for a way out to return to the estate. They go to the dark wall where at the floor level are two glowing lights, and they hear a croaking voice that says, "To seek is to find; push to whoosh." Caron sees a wedge of light; she pushes against the wall, which feels like a revolving door. With a whooshing sound, she tumbles out into the forest. Baron came out behind her.

Excitedly, they scrambled up the hill, opened the double-entry doors and turned left to the museum-like library. Where do they begin to research the meaning of all they have seen? Looking up, they notice the presence of an elderly Mr. Wentworthy in a far corner. Due to his gout, he is in an ill-humored mood. He doesn't want to hear what they have to say, but they're just so thrilled about what they found; he feels he must at least feign interest. They poured forth their fantastic tale of a toad, petroglyphs, a Kachina, and fairy dust. Even though Homer scoffs, saying, "Tut, tut, such nonsense," he is slightly curious.

After they shared everything that happened, Homer was skeptical of their story. He kindly said, "Get something to eat, a good night's rest, and tomorrow, you can show me where all this happened."

Early the following morning, the twins had Uncle Homer by the hand, leading him slowly down the hill toward the woods. "This is nonsense," Homer thought as he leaned heavily on his walking stick. With some struggle, they reached what looked like a stone wall. "This is where the door should be," said Baron. They all heard a croaking voice say, "Follow the hollow, follow the hollow." What hollow? A hollow tree, a hollow in the stone, or a hollow in the ground? Again, they heard "Follow the Hollow." Looking down, they noticed a shallow trench near their feet, which could be the hollow. It trailed toward the wall, ending in a hole underneath a big stone. Caron and Baron each tried pushing against the wall, but when Uncle Homer placed his cane into the hole, Eureka! There was the revolving door letting them into the chamber.

"I can't believe it!" exclaimed Uncle Homer. "I am astounded to find this amazing treasure in my own backyard!" Approaching the Kachina, he noticed the words, "Drink Here" and wondered where the water was. There must be codes to explain this mystery. "The wall tells all, the wall tells all." It must be that Tut. Tut the talking toad, showing us the code.

Uncle Homer sees some letters on the wall: Ka, Ra, Ya, Sa, Ta, Ha, La. They look familiar to him. He has seen them before while journeying in Egypt. "These are seed syllables," he explains to the kids. "Sounds are used to create. Perhaps we can create water here using these syllables.

Seeds carry a divine blueprint like the acorn's promise of a huge Oak tree. To understand the Creation Story of the World, we must first know that God sang it into being. For example, take the first letters of the seed syllables KRYSTHL. These spell a word sounding like crystal. KRYST sounds like Christ. This makes it all more holy, don't you think?" Caron pipes up, "I bet we have to sing these words to create the water here."

Turning around, the old man begins to examine the forms the Kachina is holding. Looking at the children, he explains, "This pyramid is called a tetrahedron and represents fire. The square pyramid that looks like a diamond is called an octahedron and represents air. You know that Plato taught in his School of Philosophy that these solid forms represent all of the planetary elements. Here is the cube associated with the earth and its four corners. Now, we have here the icosahedron, the water element. Each of its faces is triangular. The pentagonal shapes appear on the sides of the dodecahedron, looking like a miniature soccer ball. All of these forms fit inside the sphere."

"Take a chance, sing and dance, take a chance, sing and dance," croaks Tut. "Sing in a ring, Sing in a ring." Following Tut's instructions, they hold hands, forming a ring around the Kachina. Uncle Homer supplies the seed syllables of "Ka, Ra, Ya, Sa, Ta, Ha, La." which Caron inserts into them into the tune of "Ring Around the Rosie."

Tut jumps up and down, "Spin and win, win and spin." The Kachina statue begins to spin on its sphere, and faster and faster it goes, so fast that it almost disappears. Suddenly, they hear a snap, crackle, and pop. With a swoosh, the metal statue dissolves into a fountain of water which fills the basin. Billows of steam rise in pink clouds with the aroma of roses that touch the faces of the three circling figures.

"Ah, Ah, Ah," says Uncle Homer.

"Ooh, Ooh, Ooh," exclaims Caron.

"Hurray, Hurray, Hurray," shouts Baron.

The Cavern echoes, resounding repeatedly with their words singing, "Alleluia, Alleluia, Alleluia."

Tut announces, "Time to dip and sip, time to sip and dip." They all knelt down, dipped their cupped hands into the silvery pool, and sipped the water. An immense love flowed between them as their hearts opened. The sphere had turned into a crystal ball. Gazing into it, they saw the geometric forms collapsing together, one inside another like a Russian doll. Mr. Wentworthy stood up straight and tall and, in amazement, asked the children, "What just happened?"

"We created water," squealed Caron. "We cracked the code," Baron said, clapping his hands.

Uncle declared, "Yes, yes, the code; I can hardly wait to explain the code. Thank you, thank you for bringing me along on your 'Toadly Adventure.' I had lost all hope of sharing with anyone my life of travel, and the wisdom I gained seemed not to matter at all." With a broad grin, he spread his arms, and the children ran to him. They hugged all around. "Sharing is caring, caring is sharing," the twins giggled, looking at each other. "Attitude is gratitude; gratitude is attitude," gurgled Tut from the pool of water as he bobbed up; now he was smooth and beautiful, the warts were gone!

At this point, the children recognize Uncle as a teacher and begin to drown each other out with their questioning. "Hold on, hold on, not everything all at once," cautioned Uncle Homer as he guided them back to the crystal ball. At its center, there were flames of pale yellow, pink, and blue; purple and gold also appeared. "This means something, children, would you like to know? What you see here has many interpretations that differ throughout the world. There are over 7,000 languages. In order to understand one another, we must decode their signs, symbols, and words. Languages are a form of encryption, and that is what creates boundaries. Communication that includes the heart flame emanates love. Ponder if love is the glue that fixes everything. Remember, the word fixative is a synonym for glue. For example, to crystalize may mean, 'All eyes on Christ."

Why do you think messages are hidden in words? Well, messages between friends are not understood by foes when we scramble the letters."

"Did you know the word Merkaba is associated with the Seal of Solomon, in the House of David?"

The children asked, "Did you learn about this in your travels to Egypt and Israel?"

"Thank you for asking." Uncle replied, "There is so much more I could tell you, but at this point, let me emphasize the geometry behind the Merkaba. Imagine a triangle associated with the fire element igniting smaller triangles out of each side, creating the star tetrahedron. The Star Tetrahedron represents heaven and earth meeting one another. As they intersect, they form what was anciently referred to as the Chariot of Fire. Etheric fire from heaven descending and fire from the human heart ascending corresponds to Spirit connecting with matter. Ascension is the energetic essence that transforms the waters of life into Beings of Light.

We just experienced transformation, did we not?" Kachina's message indicated, drink here to be forever young.

Thoughts provide the energy for the waters of life to continue their creative process associated with hope, renewal, and eternal life."

Baron, feeling overwhelmed, looked up at his uncle and frowned, "Too much thinking makes me tired." Uncle Homer says, "So, you've had enough, have you? I have found that enough is never enough; there is always more. And I think that is a good thing. We are done for today. Let's go to lunch now. Tomorrow, we begin anew."

Chapter 20

Travis Sutton

Travis Sutton is a best-selling author, husband to Chelsea Sutton, and self-taught digital creative in ConsultMent, based out of Phoenix, Arizona. Born and raised in Farmville, North Carolina, Travis holds an accounting degree from Top 20 – WP Carey School of Business at Arizona State, and a master's degree in taxation from Top 15 – Sturm College of Law at University of Denver. In his spare time, he loves reconnecting with nature on hikes around Phoenix, connecting with his creative hobbies, playing golf and riding horses.

Website: travsutton.com
LinkedIn: linkedin.com/in/travsutton

To view our video interview with Travis, please scan the QR Code with your smartphone or go to:
https://youtu.be/OkOrrm49QnM

Where the River and Oak Meet

By Travis Sutton

"Blood may be thicker, but the bond
of friendship is stronger."
~Arthelia "Thelia" Bell

Where the River and Oak Meet

By Travis Sutton

"Don't we remember what happened in Waym's Pass, gang? I don't know if I can do that again," Thelia uttered.

She and her crew of misfits overcame a surprise attack a few days earlier when the Snake of Alcantera's men, the 2 Septeria Brothers carved from Mount Eden's ashes, set an almost perfect ambush. The misfits may have escaped with their lives and the Gem of Layl, but this quest to return the gem to the Queen of Oracle feels at the very least, daunting, and at the very most, impossible.

Coming from the North Country takes guts. It's not all rainbows and horseshoes in the snow caps and frigid tundra. But to step foot or hoof in the Serene Forest, well, you're either brave, dumb, or maybe a little of both. The evergreen Cat's Paws and Nightshade Junipers are yet to bloom, while the stunning albeit deadly Coral Ambrosia sings a lullaby of normalcy that makes this place feel like home. The River of Tsehili cascades through the southwestern corner and barrels over the Great Rim, leading to the City of Oracle by the Basin of Hoohoogam, but the forest holds its secrets well and doesn't like to kiss nor tell.

"I don't like it either, but we have to, there's no way around," Thelia said. One by one, the crew stepped foot into the forest. One, Meazel the Weasel, a cunning, small yet surprisingly trustworthy member of the Weasel clan. Two, Joffre, a loyal black dingo with hedgehog-like fur that may or may not be the life of any gathering he attends. Then there's Arthelia "Thelia" Bell. A 23-year-old, tall and lanky brunette, "Thelia" as her friends call her is no stranger to bravery. Some say it was passed down from her bloodline; after all, her mother always stood up to The Snake. Some say the Shaman of the North Country taught her his ways, but who's to say? We like to think she was born for this very moment, right here, right now.

"This definitely isn't the North Country," Joffre said as he, Meazel, and Thelia glanced at the first Coral Ambrosia on the path. Evergreens cast shadows that keep the hot sun at bay, and the chirping of the Homeric Warbler can be faintly heard from a fence post just ahead. "Not so bad, Pals," Meazel chimed, "we'll be in Oracle by sundown at this pace."

You see, what the three don't realize is there are all sorts of things awaiting. From the Algae Goop to the strongest of Bindweed, and don't get us started on George, the Cycloptic Puma that lives under the Giant Oak of the South. Will he be asleep? Will he be hungry? Nobody knows, but what we do know is this: we've got a lot of ground to cover.

Meanwhile, to the East near Wavering Lake, The Snake, a great-statured greying man with the animal of his namesake as a tattoo from shoulder to shoulder, stands over his solid medieval era round table. Before him lay the plans to finally take what he so foolishly claims to be rightfully his, the gem.

"If you two had more than one geode between you, this wouldn't need to happen," The Snake tells the Septeria Brothers. "We know," they reply in unison.

"She's in the Forest," he says. "We know," they lowly respond.

Sternly he says, "you know what this means? Don't you?" To which they utter, "uhhhhhhhh."

"Mount up, knuckleheads; we'll cut them off South of The Giant Oak. They'll be plenty tired by then, if they even make it there at all."

Back in the Forest, Thelia has led the team to a junction. To the left, a heading towards Wavering Lake, while straight ahead, a bridge comes into focus. Thelia knows that the only way to Oracle is to forge straight ahead, and so she and the misfits begin the same as when entering the forest. One step, two steps, three steps, four steps, one in front of the other over the rickety bridge that hovers mere inches over a brown goop. "This must be the algae," she says, "nobody tou-!" Blam!!! Joffre breaks through the bridge and begins sinking into the goop. Remember how we said he's the life of the party? Well, maybe he got a little too excited. "I can't get out!" he frantically yelps.

"Hold on, Joff, Thelia's coming," Meazel shouts, as there's not much a weasel that weighs 6 ounces can do in these situations. As Joffre sinks further and grasps his front paws to the side of the bridge, Thelia is reminded that she brought her father's trusted blue lasso. "Don't fail me now," Thelia whispers as she tosses it towards Joffre. A miss! Joffre slips a little further as she furls back in the line. Another toss and miss! "I can't hold onto the bridge much longer; this stuff is swallowing me!" Joffre exclaims. A rush of thoughts come to Meazel's cunning brain, "I can run the rope and tie it to him. I've seen this stuff before, and us weasels know we're lighter than the goop. We can make snow angels in this stuff."

"Let's try it," Thelia says. As Meazel takes the line out, he takes one hop on the goop, two hops on the goop, and with the third hop lands on top of Joffre's head. "I'll just tie it here, here, and maybe here, and we... are... solid," Meazel says with a smile. "Pull, Thelia, pull!" the two shout.

As Thelia finishes bringing Joffre up, he says, "Well...that wasn't that bad. Right?" They all softly chuckle, knowing these things can turn sour.

While this is the right way, seldom does that make it any easier. The crew finds themselves back in the forest amongst the Ambrosia's lulling scent and the Bindweed snapping at their heels, but at least there's a sense of normal to these elements, much more normal than being swallowed alive by goop, I suppose. "Only a few minutes to go; we have to watch for George!" Thelia tells the others.

The gang quickly arrives where the Tsehili curves around The Great Oak. "This is it! The crossing point," Thelia looks over the ledge above the mighty river.

Unfortunately for everyone, The Snake had been following the Tsehili since they left the lake, and now, as the sun sets, it's showtime in the forest.

The Septeria spot Thelia's gang up ahead breaking into a full run toward the group. You can hear these guys coming from a mile away. It could be that they're made from stone, but ballerinas at the ball they are not. Thelia, Meazel, and Joffre seem tired but are ready, game on!

As the two brothers battle Thelia, The Snake watches on in delight. He never did like to dirty his hands in these matters – he always saw himself as the "governing" type and this is one of those situations that's far below his paygrade.

"Give them everything you have, my friends!" Thelia clamors. The crew is getting pushed to the brink, and it's all they can do to hold. One Septeria fist lands cleanly on Joffre, knocking him out cold. Now it's down to Meazel and Thelia, and as we've said before, Meazel is more of a cunning mind, a lover more than a fighter. Alas, he's no use in these situations either.

With Joffre out of the way, the brothers close in on Thelia, backing her into the rocky ledge that borders the Tsehili. "I wish it wasn't this way," Thelia says as a tear rolls down her cheek.

"We still have to get to Oracle," Meazel proudly shouts. The brothers turn to the weasel's direction, only to have their confidence shed into fear. George, a nemesis of The Snake, was indeed awake, and the cunning creature that Meazel is had struck a deal for help. "So I hear the brothers are in my forest, hmmmm," George snarls, "I guess we're going to have to do something about that!" George lunges at the two brothers knocking one into the water with the initial blow. The thing about fighting next to the Tsehili, anything made from ash returns to ash when touched by the waters. The Snake is nervous.

George lunges at the second brother and becomes entangled in an intense grapple, but the tides have turned. Thelia, still in the fight, grabs one leg of the Septeria with her trusted lasso, throwing him into an off-balance stumble. With one decisive slash, George rejoins the Septeria with his brother in the river.

"I can't believe we won, I am forever grateful, George," Thelia humbly vows.

"I have one more thing to do kiddo," George turns and looks at The Snake. "Game on?" George snarls and grins as the chase ensues back towards the lake. Meanwhile, Thelia, Meazel, and the freshly awoken Joffre cross the Tsehili toward the southern bound of the Serene Forest and towards the Colossal Peregrines and Golden Bruins of The Great Rim.

Chapter 21

Viviane Chauvet

Viviane Chauvet is an advanced Arcturian Hybrid Avatar, published author, international public speaker, creator of the Arcturian Energy Matrix Healing® and the Arcturian Healing Arts Program, and owner of Infinite Healing from The Stars.

Over the past decade, Viviane has conducted 22,000 private healing sessions worldwide for transformative changes and quantum evolution. She has traveled in several countries, including Costa Rica, Egypt, and Greece, to give intergalactic lectures and co-host global gatherings. The Hopi, Zuni, and Lakota Indigenous Nations Elders have recognized Viviane as a Star Being. Her presence emanates the radiance of the Arcturus 13th Light Dimension system.

She features in a multi-award-winning documentary, "Extraordinary: The Revelations," and will feature in an upcoming documentary based on Craig Campobasso's "The Extraterrestrial Species Almanac."

Viviane's collaborative #1 Bestselling book series "Wisdom of the Silver Sisters – Guiding Grace" and "Golden Wisdom of Love, Legends & Legacies" are available on Amazon. In 2020, Viviane founded an online Community of light-minded people with exclusive memberships, online events, and retreats. She is the producer and co-host of <u>The Infinite Star Connections Podcast</u>. Follow us on YouTube, the Conscious Awakening Network (CAN), Facebook, and Patreon.

For information on Viviane's services, meditations, and program, visit our website: https://www.infinitehealingfromthestars.com/.

YouTube Channel:
https://www.youtube.com/c/VivianeChauvetGalacticHealer

Patreon Community:
https://www.patreon.com/InfiniteHealingfromtheStars

Facebook:
https://www.facebook.com/vivianechauvetgalactichealer/

Instagram:
https://www.instagram.com/viviane_chauvet/

To view our video interview with Viviane, please scan the QR Code with your smartphone or go to: https://youtu.be/5RDvPy28YJE

A Sparkle in Time

Viviane Chauvet

"The Earth laughs in flowers."
—Ralph Waldo Emerson

A Sparkle in Time

Viviane Chauvet

To write well is to write what we know. Stories interweave a multi-layered tapestry of connections that become immortalized in the memories of Time. We are the pure Essence of Divine Light expressed as fractals of light condensed in physical form. Our life journey tells the most unique tale of Soul discovery, experiences, and evolution. The utmost goal is to return to Oneness in the embrace of the Prime Creator.

For eons, our interstellar civilization has served as guardians and master teachers to numerous intelligent consciousness groups at various stages of cosmic evolution. We have traveled throughout the multiverse in the most advanced and sentient starships. After thousands of years of service to Supreme Source, we still play active roles as emissaries and ambassadors for Councils, delegations, Guardians of Time, and the Builders of Forms.

Our tale truly begins with the curiosity and the selflessness of an Avatar Soul who heard the calling of a celestial being known as planet Earth. This Avatar decided to send a soul aspect of her being through the gateway of the Star Arcturus. This gateway leads directly to the Solar System, part of the Blue Physical Plane of Existence. Our starships have specific interstellar maps of this quadrant and its orbiting planets. Even the Universal Hall of Records archives the Earth's historical timelines and evolutionary cycles. Beings of Light come to the Universal Records to review the next potential of a planet, civilization, galaxy, and more!

As the Avatar's soul aspect began its journey, the soul energy took on an identity. It embodied a physical form, allowing an in-depth exploration of dimensions and overlays of co-existing realities. She soon discovered that the Earth/Gaia has a luminous and complex grid system that creates an ecosystem for sentient life. Every person, or soul expression, projects a specific reality based on the consciousness and interpretation of experiences, belief systems, emotional and mental states, past life memories, and many other factors. Over the years, Valencia has developed her ability to communicate with higher dimensional realms and ascended beings, including Masters. Her natural capacity to hold higher frequencies has attracted an unexpected invitation to explore the Galactic Faerie realm. Their kingdom co-exists with the Earth's energetic field, only at a higher vibratory state.

7 Years with the Galactic Faery

On a sunny day in Autumn, Valencia decided to take a long walk in the forest near her house. She felt a calling to commune with the tree nations and the land. As usual, she brought a bag of almonds to share with the squirrels in preparation for winter. Valencia is incredibly attuned to the pulse of nature and everything growing and vibrating. She frequently paused to marvel at the beauty of bushes, changing leaves, flowers, and other spectacular color spectrums. The Faerie Kingdom is particularly attentive to those who wander in the woods admiring their work. The faeries and other higher-dimensional beings took a keen interest in Valencia for her natural faculty to respond with kindness and harmony to Gaia's wonders.

Her inner Avatar's spark makes her very receptive to the symbiotic synergy of nature, the elements, and all sentient life forms, including the animal kingdom.

She suddenly perceived a vibrational shift around her, as if she stepped into a parallel reality. Everything was more vibrant, conscious, and luminous, including the trees, the sound of leaves, the soil, etc. Valencia called upon her Avatar Self to recenter herself and readjust her senses. Obviously, she was in a very different world, yet it looked like the forest she was walking in a moment ago. A group of Elvish beings greeted her at a gateway's entrance, and they telepathically explained that she was invited to enter the Faerie Kingdom. Intrigued, she accepted their invitation and voluntarily entered the gateway – a dimensional doorway – to another world!

The key element is to accept their invitation willingly. When interacting with higher-dimensional beings, one learns that their perception and codes of ethics vary greatly from those who perceive reality through third-frequency mental and limited filters. In other words, your state of consciousness will determine your capacity to perceive and interact with other multi-dimensional intelligence. Everything must be a positive vibrational match to co-exist in the same resonance field.

What Valencia learned is truly beyond words. She developed the ability to set the sun, speak sacred tones, commune with many beings in their native vibrational languages, access sacred archives, dance and sing in ways that defy the law of gravity, and much more! She was becoming part of their tribe, one of them, and she experienced love in its purest form. Her entire light body was shimmering with color frequencies unknown to the perceived light spectrum.

Although Valencia's blueprint contained the light codes and gifts of her new abilities, she could only access them in the presence of the faeries and the elvish groups. Every experience became an opportunity to shift consciousness and accelerate Valencia's personal evolution. Since the Faerie Kingdom abides by the Universal Laws, time is perceived and experienced much faster than on the third-dimensional linear time construct. Each month spent in their realm equated to a year of experiences and knowledge for Valencia.

After nearly a year (quantified in 3D linear time), Valencia had stayed seven years in the company of the Faeries and other dimensional beings like the Elves, Gnomes, etc. The symbolic number 7 is highly meaningful to them, representing a sacred cycle of evolution. The Elves explained that if Valencia stayed any longer among them, the portal between their dimensions would close, meaning she would never return to her physical reality. Because Valencia's Soul Akashic Records show that her Avatar's soul essence came to directly assist other life forms to evolve back to the fifth dimension, the Faerie High Council decided to return Valencia to her original path and, therefore, closed the portal.

Even though she would no longer be able to cross their gateway, she retained all the knowledge, virtues, and most sacred memories of her incredible journey. Naturally, many of them still visit her from time to time. In most of her travels, Valencia can detect the presence of an energetic opening to the Faerie Kingdom. Whenever they are around, she sees and feels their presence. Let your heart be at peace because we are, after all, interconnected by the unified field of Oneness!

Treasured Memories...

Legacy

"I saw grief drinking a cup of sorrow and called out,
"It tastes sweet does it not?"
'You've caught me,' grief answered,'
and you ruined my business.
How can I sell sorrow, when you know it's a blessing?"

~Rumi

Chapter 22

Betsy Brill

Betsy Brill was among the first to receive the polio vaccine in the 1950s and possibly the most eager for COVID-19 vaccines in 2021. She's a former journalist, editor, and publication designer. With two women friends, Betsy co-founded HandUp Congo, a tiny non-profit aiding women in the Democratic Republic of Congo. She is an aspiring clay sculptor.

Betsy lives in San Francisco and Scottsdale, Arizona, where her daughter resides. She and her family adopted Tom Brown, who advised them to blow bubbles with a straw if chocolate in an iced mocha is not well mixed. In Tom's memory, they now blow bubbles just for the fun of it.

www.handupcongo.org
www.facebook.com/betsybrill
www.ourplaceinprovence.com
Betsyb123@mac.com
PO Box 15306, San Francisco, CA 94115

To watch our video interview with Betsy, please scan the QR Code below or go to this link: https://youtu.be/51QsRia18XE

Gratitude for Having Known Him

By Betsy Brill

Ntafendaka ntando la mpos'e'ola!
"One does not cross a river by merely longing for home."
~Congolese proverb

Gratitude for Having Known Him

by Betsy Brill

*"I have lived long enough to know that most of the things
I worried about never happened, that most of the things
I felt bad about turned out for the better,
and that most of the things I hoped would stay the same
couldn't stay the same if they wanted to,
because change is the process of life itself."*

Tom Brown
5/25/1932—10/10/2023

During the seven years that Tom Brown graced my life, I loved him like another father and witnessed his lasting impact on everyone who met him – whether in person or on Facebook (where 1000 friends remarked on his thoughtful essays, groaned at his silly puns, and engaged in the word games he posted). I loved punning with him, even though he ALWAYS got in the last groan.

I've heard him described as kind to the core. And he was.

I knew he'd been in prison, as I'd met him through a prison re-entry advocacy organization. He'd been released after 14 years behind bars for financial fraud. He had experienced the re-entry maze that is seemingly designed to lead right back to prison. Having successfully navigated it, he was there to help others.

He was grey-haired and wizened. His eyes were kind and sometimes tired. His voice was soft-spoken. He was subtlety and uproariously funny when he mused his word games aloud. As I came to know him, I learned that he was far more than all that.

He had a degree in English Literature from Ohio State University. He wrote essays every day while he was in prison. He'd fallen in love with Blue Grass music when he was still in high school, and even invited Bill Monroe, who created the sound, to be interviewed on the school radio station.

I found a dog-eared photo of Tom and his beloved Annie Eveland with Bill Monroe among his few remaining belongings. There was also his 1955 Air Force yearbook, where the expression he was known for was noted: "Well, I don't know now."

I'd often heard him use those exact words.

And I realized that his passion for punning had long preceded the history he shared with me. I found his personal "punnery" book, printed on a dot-matrix printer. And during the last of his days, he asked for his notebooks in which he perfected his word games and puns in his careful script.

I knew that he had spent seven years as an Air Force pilot before moving to Phoenix, where he became a mega-successful real estate investor. He and Annie often hosted musical gatherings at their home.

He was a talented guitarist and singer himself. They traveled to see Bill Monroe, Johnny Cash, and others perform live over their three decades together. When he was alive, he wouldn't let me share that he had even jammed with some of them after performances. He didn't want anyone to think he was something he wasn't.

And he told me how his successful former life ended almost 20 years before I met him.

He and his fellow real estate investors — many of them friends — had been caught in a collapsing real estate market.

Convinced the market would soon recover, he encouraged more backers to invest with him — to buy time and to help cover earlier investors' losses.

His timing was several years off.

Prosecutors called the resulting financial implosion Tom Brown's pyramid scheme. "I knew what I was doing was wrong," he recalled sadly, "but I was just so sure I could make us all whole again."

He faced multiple counts of fraud – millions of dollars in value had disappeared—and with it, investors' money.

The man who hadn't known where the jail was located now entered its frightening confines to await trial.

"I knew I would lose everything. I knew I was going to prison. But the thought of my friends' losses was what was unbearable," he told me. "I didn't know how to handle what was happening to my life. The future was so uncertain, so frightening.

"I decided to commit myself to being a loving presence."

I wanted to know what happened to a loving presence in the company of wily thieves, drug-dealing addicts, violent gang members, and hardened criminals. He chuckled as he told me.

That first day in jail, during lunch time, a tattooed bull of a man thundered about the room in a rage. The fearsome giant bellowed at first one man and then another about the "animals" they were eating. They should NOT be eating animal flesh. The thought, let alone the sight, of an outraged vegetarian sermonizing inmates in a jailhouse cafeteria was surreal. I could see it all unfold in my mind's eye.

The timid newcomer, too fearful to say a word to any of the surly, rough-looking crowd, finally spoke up when the huge man approached him.

The silver-haired new inmate quietly responded to the irate man with a question. "Well, then how do you feel about animal crackers?"

The bellowing giant stopped dead and just stared at Tom. Unmanly giggles tittered throughout the room, followed by outright guffaws.

"What did you say to me?" the angry hulk demanded, his voice low and measured.

"How do you feel about animal crackers?" Tom repeated solemnly. An unwilling smile slipped across the giant's face as his joined the laughter filling the room.

"When those men cracked up, releasing their own tensions, perhaps fears, I fully understood the power of laughter to soothe, maybe to heal."

Tom Brown's mission of love launched with laughter.

Most of Tom's friends forgave him despite their enormous losses. But banks, financial institutions, and the law demanded justice and restitution. Everything he owned would be confiscated and sold to help repay his investors. When it was all gone, he still owed millions in restitution, a debt impossible to ever repay.

His biggest regret, he told me before he died, was how Annie had been caught unaware and had been harassed even though he'd never shared any of his business dealings with her.

While behind bars, Tom earned 50 cents an hour preparing men to take the GED. The conservative white businessman mixed for the first time in his sheltered life with people of all colors, all religions, all backgrounds, of every economic stratum. He saw first-hand the tragedy of low self-esteem, the lasting impact of poor education. He came to understand how poverty, abandonment, and abuse, nourished by poor judgment and ignorance, could germinate into crime. Most people in prison have committed illegal acts, he saw, but they weren't all the inherently bad people the kind, but privileged, white man expected to encounter there.

Perhaps it was his age, he told me, that protected him from the violence he feared, though he did witness violence. Perhaps it was the respect he showed to every man, guard, or inmate. Perhaps it was his sense of humor. Perhaps, he once mused with sadness, it was because the size of his restitution was so impressive.

Before every class, teacher Tom wrote a joke or pun on the blackboard. The men and he laughed a lot in his classroom. The guards soon began popping in for their own daily chuckles.

His journey to prison was the first he had ever made without a dog at his side. His last dog, a Cocker Spaniel, died shortly before Tom was sentenced. "It was as if he knew he wouldn't be able to come along."

Tom told me that his invisible dog Ralphie was born of the need for a canine companion — and of the desire to create more laughter for his students. In addition to puns on the blackboard, the students began encountering a different drawing of Ralphie every day.

And a jubilant Ralphie decorated every assignment that earned an A. "Way to go," Ralphie might declare. "Good job!"

"I'll never forget the day I was handing out diplomas," he told me. "One inmate refused to accept his unless I drew Ralphie on the certificate. I told him that a diploma is an official document and that I wasn't sure I should do that."

The man persisted. "Ralphie got me through this. Ralphie needs to help me celebrate!" Tom drew a proud Ralphie on the diploma.

Tom walked out of prison an 80-year-old man with $50 in his pocket, every penny earned while inside. He no longer described himself as conservative.

Another Vietnam veteran volunteering with the VA helped him find transitional housing. He was grateful to finally rent a 425-square-foot Section 8 apartment where the manager overlooked his criminal record and his only income, monthly Social Security benefits. Bringing along Ralphie the invisible dog was not a problem.

Reflecting at 90 about his long life, Tom said without hesitation that his 13 years in prison were the most important to him. Not his happy childhood, not his military service, not his wild business successes. Not even traveling the nation to see heroes like Bill Monroe, Willie Nelson, Johnny Cash, or other big-name musicians perform live.

Society's broken men — his fellow human beings of all classes, races, and colors behind bars had made him a wiser man, a better human being able to see beyond society's surface. He became filled with compassion, love — and gratitude.

"When you have nothing and are living in gratitude," he said, "you realize that even a little is enough."

***

Ultimately, what I learned from Tom is that what others experience as another's genuine kindness can be the profound impact of a life lived in gratitude.

During the final two years of his life, Tom experienced a series of health crises from falls and breaks to various infections that sent him into hospitals and skilled nursing centers, back to his tiny studio, then back to the hospital, then to another recovery center.

Through it all, he continued to be a loving presence. One after another of the people who cared for him marveled at his kindness and gentle sense of humor. When it was time for his release, they weren't ready for him to leave.

"I so appreciate you," he told each person who helped him, from the person who brought his food to the person who cleaned him when he soiled himself. "Thank you so, so much."

"No one ever told me that before," was, too often, their shared response.

He was ready to "go," he told his closest friends during the last two months of his life. At 91+, he could see a future of more doctor appointments, waiting rooms, hospital stays, and weeks in recovery centers. He was experiencing confusion and loss of autonomy. Everything was overwhelming him.

"I've lost my joy," he said, "I never thought I'd lose my joy."

He finally moved into a small group assisted living home, where he was lovingly cared for by a gentle young man for the two weeks that turned out to be the rest of his life.

The last time I saw him, he was in good spirits, and told me that he had always been the the kind of person who needed to have control —that he had been overwhelmed because he had no control. He had awakened that day, he stated with an exclamation point, and had simply released control. He no longer felt like "checking out," a term he'd used often in the previous two months. He was filled with gratitude for the home where he was living, and especially for the young man who was his primary caretaker. He felt his joy returning, he told me.

In fact, we joyfully planted a whoopy cushion in the comfortable chair in which his frequent visiting friends would sit. He was almost gleeful in anticipation of laughs to come.

He couldn't wait to tell me after his friend Dan's visit for a Sunday Zoom meeting with their friends, a meeting called "Male Meanderings." Dan had plopped into the chair and gone wide-mouthed at the startling, sputtering loud sounds.

The only thing, Tom lamented to me, was that the fellas were already at the Zoom meeting when Dan sat down, and that we'd have to figure out something else for them!

Two mornings later, following a good night's sleep and having been cleaned up and dressed by his young caretaker, he joined the rest of the household at breakfast. He then collapsed and died.

**

Having known Tom during his most recent lifetime, I came to understand how deep his heart had always been, when Annie, the love of his life, shared with me this song he had written during yet another lifetime.

The Call of Spirit, by Tom Brown

The Truth within, I hear it whisper.
My thoughts, unbound by habit's chains,
Tell me that good and evil labels
Are only love and fear with different names.

Chorus:
The call of Spirit how it taunts me.
How it echoes down the canyons of my soul.
The call of spirit how it haunts me.
I'm so different from the me I used to be.

My understanding drifts yet higher
Like a bird just trying out new wings.
The embers rise up from truth's fire.
My spirit soars now free of earthly things.

Chorus:
The call of spirit how it taunts me,
As it echoes down the canyons of my soul.
The call of spirit how it haunts me.
I'm so different from the me I used to know.

Says Annie, "That is where we find the essence of his spirit, the deeper connection. I wondered why I was recently thinking of 'his song' – the one he wrote many years ago, and yet seemed so much more fitting… now.

"Perhaps we all in subtle, profound ways prepare for our passing into spirit. Perhaps in some astounding moments, we realize the incredible spirits that we are. I believe he did."

Chapter 23

Love Letter

Jody: December 29, 1947 - August 25, 2018
Jonita Kay Foster Jones' Love Letter.
Dictated by Jody on August 15, 2018
Transcribed by her loving cousin Sharyn G. Jordan

"Everyone was always welcome at Jody's kitchen table. We delighted in such sumptuous meals: her famous peach cobbler topped with French vanilla ice cream served with her bottomless CUPPA-strong coffee and robustly enriching conversations. Jody's Texas tea (Aunt Nita's recipe) was perfect, as were the bowls of delectable, hand-snapped black-eyed peas with a sublime side, a 'just out of the oven,' generous slice of buttered, sweet cornbread. Joy, laughter, light, and love warmed our hearts and will forever inspire us."

Sharyn G. Jordan-McWhorter
Sister/Cousins. BFF's,
& their precious Granny Kincannon GRAND-Girls

To my precious family and friends, thank you seems too little to say yet, from my heart to yours, please know how much I love & appreciate you.

Indeed, I was given the gift of extra time which I now know was actually only borrowed. During those health challenges, my precious family rallied around me especially my beloved husband Bobby of fifty-two years and my sweet baby sister Lindy who temporarily 'moved in' with us from her Alaskan home of thirty years. They continue to be my Earth Angels.

I even spent this past summer swimming, having quality of time with my beautiful Grand Daughters Haylie, Maddie & Macy and being ever so grateful for my infinite blessings. However, the end of July, an excruciating lower back & hip pain determined the Cancer had returned with a vengeance. This time it had already consumed my lungs, liver, hip socket and lymph glands. My dearest loved ones, my time in this wonder-filled world is expiring.

Compassionately and necessarily, my long time Dr. Patel ordered Hospice. I am surrounded and enfolded in the bosom of my home and family. Yes, my emotions are widely ranged however, the one that is closest to my soul is PEACE. This makes my writing to you so much easier. Life's one common certainty is our journey home. Oh, what a comfort to know my place in Glory-Land is reserved. At times, I can already see my Welcoming Committee gathering at St. Peter's pearly gates.

LOVE LETTER

One of the requests I have of you is to continue to love on and support one another. As my trusted Dr. Patel encouraged, "Jonita Jones, Keep Living." Therefore, I am not dying. I am choosing to live every day to the fullest of my abilities. Lovingly, we will keep your posted on my circumstances and we welcome visitors at any time.

The following poem inspires me as I ask you to think of each of your loved ones gone before you in this matter. I know I do. Written by Henry Scott Holland (l,1.27.1847-3.17.1918, Professor of Divinity oat the University of Oxford, it is as follows:

DEATH IS NOTHING AT ALL
~Henry Scott-Holland

Death is nothing at all.
It does not count.
I have only slipped away into the next room.
Nothing has happened.

Everything remains exactly as it was.
I am I, and you are you,
and the old that we lived so fondly together,
is untouched, unchanged.
Whatever we were to each other,
that we are still.

Call me by the old familiar name.
Speak of me in the easy way which you always used.
Put no difference into your tone.
Wear no forced air of solemnity or sorrow.

Laugh as we always laughed at the little jokes
that we enjoyed together.
Play, smile, think of me, pray for me.
Let my name be ever the household word that it always was.

Let it be spoken without an effort, without the
ghost-brethren of a shadow upon it.

Life means all that it ever meant.
It is the same as it ever was.
There is absolute and unbroken continuity.
What is death but a negligible accident?

Why should I be out of mind because I am out of sight?
I am but waiting for you, for an interval.
Somewhere very near, just round the corner.

All is well.
Nothing is hurt. Nothing is lost.
One brief moment and all will be as it was before.
How we shall laugh at the trouble of parting, when we meet again."

Good Grief

By Mardette "Mardy Bee" Burr

Sometimes life can be so ironic.

I chose to use my wedding photograph for this piece here, and yet I am having to write about my dear husband's death. This just puts me in the place of the ying and the yang, and to the start and to the end of it all.

What can I say, the fact is that my whole world as I knew it, has been completely turned upside down.

Sadly, my sweet husband Chris passed away only thirty-two days ago. He was diagnosed with a very rare and aggressive form of cancer, and he lived for approximately twenty-seven days after he was diagnosed with this terminal and awful disease.

I'm not going to lie this has been one of the most difficult things that I have ever had to go through in my entire life. "Good grief" is all that I can say!

Right now, I feel like I am living in a sort of a palindrome world. I feel very emotionally RAW, and I also feel like I am raging from a WAR.

Palindrome RAW in the fact that all of my senses just seem to be on such an edge.

WAR in the fact that I feel like I am having to battle so many different things right now.

I've got to admit that this internal and external RAW WAR is currently wreaking havoc on my innards, and in my outward appearance too. I've been crying so much and so hard sometimes over the most basic and simple things. I've genuinely connected with others who are experiencing the same thing.

Nowadays, sometimes my stomach feels all right, and then on other days I feel like I can barely get down a bite.

And all the things that I've had to deal with all ready, would make a strong person grow weak in the knees.

Here's some of the war-like battles I've had to fight already since my husband's demise. I swear you can't make things like this up.

- Somehow, I was locked out of our bank account when the Social Security office deposited and then withdrew my husband's monthly pension check.

- Next, I got a notice in the mail that our car insurance was going to be cancelled due to non-payment of the bill. Apparently, a billing notice was sent to my husband's e-mail account about this, and I never even knew about it. Once I found out about this, I called them and immediately made a payment to them.
- Because my husband died on the 30th of the month, I lost my health insurance coverage on that day. It took two weeks' time to get my health insurance coverage back on track again, with his former employer. That was a very scary time for me, because in addition to my husband's death, I myself, have recently been diagnosed with breast cancer as well.
- I had to make sure that I had health insurance coverage to be able to carry on with my own cancer journey now.
- For some reason, accounts listed in his name are not being paid by the bank now, even though his debit card is still active and alive and is still connected to our joint bank account. For no reason yesterday our internet was cut off. I called the company yesterday and discovered that our bill was not paid directly from our bank account, like it has been in the past. So, I had to go down there today, and put the account in my name, and I had to get a new router box.
- Since the Internet was out, it messed with our Ring Camera in the front and the back of the house. I now have to go in and try to re-program that so it will work again,
- Additionally, our washer wouldn't drain, and I had to call a Washer Repairman to get that fixed. Then the check Brake Light came on in the car, and I had to go deal with that too.

I swear this list just goes on and on… Black mold was discovered in our house, so I've been working on that too!

At this point, I've just held up my hands and said, "what else can you give me now?" It's almost become a comedy of errors of all of the things that I have had to go through in this past month.

The best advice I can give to anyone is to make sure that you have enough money in your account(s) to get you by, because various forms of income will immediately stop.

This is why I chose to title this work "Good Grief" because there really is a lot of BS that you have to go through and put up with, when someone you love and you know dies. It's very trying, it's very difficult, it's very tiring, and it's extremely overwhelming too! There's nothing passive about this. Dealing with death is a very hard and moving thing to do!

'Good grief,' so how does one learn how to cope? I think that it has a lot to do with how much SELF CARE that someone is able to give to themselves. I have discovered that now is not the time to push myself. Plenty of rest is in order and is very much needed. Staying hydrated, eating nutritionally, and nourishing one's spiritual soul seems to be in order now.

I try to wake up every day and start my day with thoughts and prayers of positivity and hope!

- I've humbly prayed, and I've cried a lot, a lot!
- I've reached out to others as best as I can.
- I've asked for hugs as needed, and I've even connected with strangers in this particular kind of way! What a treat!
- Additionally, I've gotten into my "comfort drawer" that I have, and I've picked out a special treat just for myself… Just a little something to make me smile bigger and better.
- I treated myself to a massage one day, after all of the phone calls that I had to make in regard to my husband's death that day.
- I've literally forced myself to get out of the house, at least once a week.
- I've gone to a concert solo, and out to dinner with my family and friends.

- I went and hung out at my favorite coffee and wine bar, and also went to a play by myself.
- I've taken rides out into the country and even went on a back road adventure by myself. Right now, I am trying to do everything that I can for self-comfort. Chris and I were married for thirty-two years.

Does this feel weird? I'm not going to lie to you, it most certainly does.

To calm myself, I have watched and laughed at some majorly funny movies. I've also taken time for my prayer and meditation, lit a lovely, scented candle, and warmly percolated inside the hot tub.

I've spent a lot more time with my precious pups and have joyfully smiled when I have taken them for a ride in the car. It's just so nice, they have now become my protective comforters when we all connectively snuggle at night now.

I love nature and I try to get out in it every single day! I take lovely photos, do lots of deep breathing exercises, and tend to post some very positive quotes.

"Good Grief!"

Can it really be? I think with a little help and guidance, that it can be. The good things that have come out of my husband's death is that I am comforted in the fact, that my husband is no longer in any sort of pain, and he is not suffering anymore!

Through his death I have been able to connect with a lot of old friends from my past. And I must say that I enjoyed that very much.

I feel so blessed to have heard so many nice words about my husband Chris. He truly was a good guy who was loved by many, both near and far! I feel very grateful that I was able to help him through this extremely difficult time in his life! He truly was at peace and he was comforted.

The next night after he was terminally diagnosed and told that he was going to be put in Hospice Care, we stayed up late into the night and talked. We talked about a saying that I had learned about, from an old friend of mine who was a Life Coach. Her method of thinking was this. She said that 'whenever someone is faced with any sort of major decision or problem, they basically have three different choices in life. And that is to Accept it, Change it, or Leave it.'

Chris and I talked deep into the night. By this time his cancer had spread so sadly far!

He said "I feel like this is my fate. I've had cancer twice before. I can't leave it and I can't change it, so the only thing left for me to do is to "accept it." Wow, talk about some heroic bravery! I know that this was a big decision on his part! And yet, deep down in our hearts we knew that it was the right decision for us.

After that, Chris fought very valiantly and very bravely as best as he could. He stayed up for long days, visited and talked with his family and friends. He enjoyed looking at old photographs, and relished sitting in the beautiful natural area where we live. He became quieter in his thoughts. And through his spiritual practices, I could see that he was trying to be more at peace, and through our own conversations I knew that he was!

Just twenty-seven days after Chris was diagnosed with a rare and aggressive form of cancer, he passed away gently and peacefully in his sleep. Both the dogs and I were with him in our room when he passed away.

Accept it, Change it, or Leave it. Can it really be that simple? Having gone through all of what I've gone through in the recent past, I have to say yes it really can be that simple and it is.

In deep contemplation, I have realized that as much as I would like to, I cannot change this situation. Through this very gut-wrenching illness I've had to come to the conclusion that my husband Chris is permanently gone. And as much as I would love it if he would walk through the door, I have whole heartily had to realize that he won't be coming back. He is now permanently gone.

Accept it, Change it, or Leave it. Faced with my own cancer journey now, I feel like I have to accept this as my own fate now too. I can't leave it, and I can't change it, so the best that I can do is to try and accept and to move on.

This is the balance of the ying and yang and of the beginning of the start to the end. The RAW WAR after death that festers within.

Accept it, Change it, or Leave it. With our palms wide open, both Chris and I have decided to embrace the divine and to love in the light. Can it really be that simple?

'Good grief,' after all that we've been through, I have to believe in the source, that says that we humbly can.

Written In Memory of my husband

Christopher A. Burr 1959 – 2024
Rest in Paradise Now

I Love and Miss You!
Mardy

World Builders

"Do not let the hero in your soul perish in lonely
frustration for the life you deserved and have never
been able to reach. The world you desire can be
won. It exists.. it is real. It is possible, it is yours."

~Ayn Rand
Atlas Shrugged

Chapter 25

Brian Dygert

Brian Dygert, born in 1959 in Illinois, grew up in Western New York as the son of a veterinarian, and the grandson of a Standardbred horseman.

Brian has a B.S. in Animal Science, NCSU and an Executive MBA, CTU. Brian created an entire career and lifestyle around the reining horse business, beginning as a professional horse trainer & producing national horse show competitions, then officiating and managing world-class equine facilities, such as Westworld of Scottsdale.

After spending 35 years judging and developing officiating training programs, he retired his judging licenses and closed his tenure on facility management to launch a consultancy and podcast, The Cowboy Office.

Now, Brian offers his expertise to venues, national and international events and listeners by conducting unorthodox data and strategic analysis of event activity and competition, all with the purpose of aiding the horse industry in growth, and helping to welcome more people to get involved with horses. The Cowboy Office can be heard on all main podcast platforms in both audio and video form.

Brian truly believes horses are good for people, as they give to us unconditionally, if we take time to ride, listen and learn. A fervent advocate, he knows that the cowboy/cowgirl way of life is good for humanity.

CONTACT INFORMATION
Brian Dygert
Brian@CowboyOffice.com

Website:
CowboyOffice.com

Social:
Facebook: https://www.facebook.com/cowboyofficeshow
Instagram: https://www.instagram.com/cowboyofficeshow
LinkedIn: https://www.linkedin.com/company/cowboy-office

Chapter 26

Daria Brill

Daria Brill has a BA in Childhood Development and an MS in Addiction Counseling. She is a counselor at the Arizona Women's Recovery Center in Phoenix.

She is also an experienced addict living in grateful recovery.

She and her parents are a tight, loving family. They continue to grow together every day. Patches, her little dog, and Tabitha and Scooter, her two finicky cats, make up her lively household.

To watch our video interview with Daria, scan the QR Code with your smartphone or go to:
https://youtu.be/Db8Xp*CGXr1E*

Not a Fairy Tale

by Daria Brill

"Nothing is impossible. Even the word says, 'I'm possible."
—Audrey Hepburn

Once upon a time, there was an intense, powerful love affair.

The difference between this one and others that come to mind is the partners in the relationship. One lover was human. The other was a synthetic substance created by other humans.

The human had started it all with a flirtation, a distraction from the pain that life can throw one's way. But the synthetic lover had taken many lovers before her and was experienced. And cruel. Very.

In the euphoria of their initial attraction, the human didn't realize the synthetic lover was feeding her long-engrained insecurities and fears while starving her spiritually, emotionally, and physically. She realized too late that her lover was devouring her soul.

The sly seductor demanded she sever ties to family and friends, slice off spiritual connections and compromise her integrity and love of humanity — at the risk of her very life. The lover waited confidently as the human's spirit broke.

As her attraction overwhelmed her, the naïve human became detached from reality. Her lover wove its way into her heart and soul, whisper by deadly whisper: "You are mine; without me you are nothing; it's too late for you; you know I can help ease you into the perpetual darkness you deserve."

The destructive affair ended not by divine force, but when I was captured by the police force in a sweep of meth addicts and sellers. My lover had so clouded my morals and values that I had turned to selling methamphetamines to support my habit.

In my addiction, I didn't feel like I was hurting others. Of course, I was destroying not just my own life, but the lives of my customers. I was a mindless addict racing as fast as I could on the drug's motorized treadmill. I was running for my life. In that frantic pursuit, I had completely alienated my family and friends.

My arrest stopped the wheel abruptly, saved my life, and allowed me an opportunity to reclaim my family and friends.

I share my story not to glamorize the chaos that led to my arrest but to share hope with those in the throes of addiction, to offer empathy and understanding to the families who I pray will not give up but will walk thru this painful journey with their loved ones.

I served five years in the Arizona Department of Corrections. There is much truth in the saying "Don't judge a book by its cover." To this day people are shocked when they learn about my past. It's as real as the Inmate number assigned to me when I became the property of the State of Arizona.

During my addiction, I had pushed my parents away with the countless poor choices I made. I am eternally grateful that they did not give up on me. My cruel lover's lies had insisted they would.

Our reconciliation did not happen easily. What changed was me.

Deep down I was relieved I had been arrested and that I was forced into abstinence. Once freed from my lover's demands — my disease — the real Daria found her way back. I served my time with intention. I got involved in every available opportunity to better myself and use my time wisely.

I found the life stories of the women around me fascinating, devastating. I began to interview my fellow inmates, who shared their traumas with me. I saw and felt their traumas. And I recognized what incredible resilience within victims of trauma.

I did not realize I was setting the stage for my future.

Unlike countless others — I was received by a loving family when I was released in 2016. They helped me transition back into society. But the bachelor's degree I had earned with the goal of becoming an elementary school teacher had been rendered useless by my felony. My future looked bleak.

I was grateful to get admin jobs in the air conditioning business for three years, though I found no joy in any of them.

Confident because I had kicked the drugs, I tested my addictive nature with drinking alcohol.

My predictable failure resulted in a DUI. My mother dropped me off at my first AA meeting because my car had been confiscated. I immediately found my home there and began anew to change my life.

Unhappy in the air conditioning business, I reviewed my passions with my father. I realized that my own recovery was my central passion. I sought and obtained a job at a substance abuse treatment center to test myself. A year later, I enrolled in a master's program for Addiction Counseling.

I graduated in July 2023 and now have the honor of serving the very population that had included me before I embarked on my own recovery.

Space does not allow tracking my years up to, in prison and beyond, but I want to honor one person — Sue Ellen Allen. Sue Ellen introduced a leadership program, Athena Within, to the women in my "yard," as the prison facility in which we lived was known.

Sue Ellen would become interwoven with my future and bless me with friendships for which I am eternally grateful. When she passed in February 2021, she was more than a mentor. She became an adopted family member and introduced me to some of the most amazing humans I've ever met, including my cherished friend, Tom Brown.

This book includes a chapter about him: "Gratitude for Having Known Him."

Sue Ellen's husband, David, and Tom Brown had been dear friends. The trio was loving and tight. When David passed, and three pals became two, Sue Ellen and Tom became the best of friends themselves.

Tom had already become my good friend when Sue Ellen asked me to look after him when she realized she was so ill that she would be leaving us. Tom and I became inseparable, too. How lucky was I?

The world feels heavy these days, so I'll close with something Tom and I discussed often before his recent death.

May we all strive to be the best versions of ourselves, remember to laugh, to be grateful — and when we do fall short, to remember that we are doing the best we can in that moment. And above all, we must always seek to be of service to others.

Chapter 27

Jessica Robinson Reissner

Upon obtaining my master's degree in mental health counseling, my journey led to working primarily with children who have experienced unimaginable abuse.

Animal rehabilitation is another cornerstone of our healing ranch, where we provide a haven for animals in need of care. This gives children and families the opportunity to witness resilience, compassion, and the profound ability to heal. Animals express unconditional love and an innate capacity to connect with our essence.

In addition, I explored the realm of metaphysical healing through crystals. These beautiful mineral combinations purify, balance, and realign our bioenergetic systems, promoting mental well-being, tranquility, positivity, focus, and even enhanced immunity and pain relief.

The unique blend of therapeutic services, including mental health therapy, compassionate animal rehabilitation, sustainable organic gardening, transformative animal healing, and the ancient wisdom of crystal healing, aims to empower individuals, especially children and their families, on a journey of holistic health.

Our ranch is a refuge that provides a safe, supportive, and inclusive space where individuals can tap into their innate power to heal and thrive. Our mission is to change the world, one child, one family, and one person at a time, by nurturing the seeds of empathy, compassion, and well-being.

CONTACT INFO:
jreissner07@gmail.com

Business: Moonpearl's Collection

Facebook: https://www.facebook.com/groups/900409833915643

Regarding the image on Jessica's chapter:

Smoky Quartz 🔥

Flames are carved into the shape of fire and flames – one of the strongest and most fascinating and mesmerizing elements known to man. With its incredible energy fire brings life and death, igniting energy into all it surrounds or touches. Similarly, crystal Flames inspire Kundalini energy enabling the user to manifest their desires, and to reach deep into themselves to find assertiveness and to beat procrastination.

Smoky quartz meaning signifies stability and grounding, so much so that the crystal is called the "grounding stone."

Smoky quartz meaning and origins stem from many cultures. Did you know that smoky quartz is the national gem of Scotland? It's no surprise, then, that this smoky crystal quartz is a prominent fixture of Celtic legend and lore. In fact, smoky quartz was sacred to the Druids, or "knowers of the oak tree," wise priests, teachers, judges, and prophets in higher ranking class systems.

In Scottish lore, Druids forged connections to the higher powers of the natural and spiritual realm. But smoky quartz isn't only sacred to Scottish folklore and legend. In mythology, the stone is associated with the ancient Greek goddess of magic, Hecate. It also represents the dark powers of Earth gods and goddesses.

Let go and ground yourself with smoky quartz, a balancing and grounding stone known for its ability to help you rise above challenging circumstances and experiences.

As the grounding stone, smoky quartz offers security and a sense of stability during times of adversity. Smoky quartz gains its grounding properties due to its close connection with the First Chakra, the Root Chakra.

Smoky quartz is a supportive healing aid that helps you let go of the past and move confidently toward a brighter future.

~Simply Divine~

Moon Pearl

By Jessica Robinson Reissner

I entered this world with eagerness and curiosity in the early days of December in Moab, Utah. My birth was an extraordinary moment, with my grandmother and aunt stepping in as midwives to welcome me into the world. From the beginning of life, I was surrounded by love and a solid foundation as my parents worked hard to provide for our family.

As a child, I was often described as an "old soul" or "born knowing." My mother thought of me as a Fairy, a magical Wood

Sprite who cared for animals, nature, and family; an insatiable thirst for knowledge accompanied my deep sense of wisdom. I would devour any book I could find, spend long hours in the school library, and research topics that piqued my interest. This pursuit of knowledge continued into my adulthood, where I felt a calling to help others. I was resolute in making a difference. I accelerated my education, graduated from high school early, and ultimately obtained my master's degree in mental health counseling.

I firmly believe that children hold the key to shaping the future. From a young age, I understood that one generation of healthy, empathetic children could positively transform the world. With this conviction, I set out to change this world one child, person, and family at a time. Diligently, I worked to earn my independent state license in professional counseling.

Empathy, I found, was at the core of emotional intelligence, and it became a cornerstone of my work with children. I discovered its transformative power, a quality that I felt compelled to instill in these young minds. Nurturing the seeds of understanding, compassion, and well-being is essential to promote mental well-being, tranquility, positivity, focus, and enhanced immunity. Teaching the children to recognize and manage their own feelings and responding to others' emotions was a powerful tool in their healing journey.

I observed a growing need for deeper connections and healing options. Through my work, I integrated alternative methods to elevate the healing process. I delved into metaphysical healing through the mineral kingdom. Working with crystals and witnessing these ancient tools' positive impact on my practice was profound. Crystals offered a unique solution with their centuries-old tradition of manifesting and healing. These beautiful mineral combinations purified, balanced, and realigned one's bioenergetic systems, promoting mental well-being, tranquility, positivity, focus, and enhanced immunity and pain relief.

But my journey didn't stop there. Animal rehabilitation is another cornerstone of our compassionately healing mission. I introduced it within counseling, bridging the gap between children and the natural world. This connection with animals made children feel grounded and secure, even in challenging circumstances. Recognizing animals' unconditional love and innate ability to connect with our essence was pivotal in healing. This allows children and families to witness resilience, compassion, and the profound ability to begin healing.

My ultimate intention, goal, and vision is to establish a ranch where we provide a haven for animals needing care. It will also allow children and families to witness resilience. In addition to our ranch being a refuge for animals in need of care, we offer the children and families an opportunity to witness resilience, compassion, and the profound ability to heal. The bond between these children and the animals they care for will become a source of strength and understanding, reminding them of the power of empathy and connection.

The unique blend of therapeutic services, including mental health therapy, compassionate animal rehabilitation, transformative animal healing, and the ancient wisdom of crystal healing, aims to empower individuals, especially children and their families, on a holistic health journey. Our ranch will be a refuge providing a safe, supportive, and inclusive space where individuals can tap into their innate power to heal and thrive.

The healing ranch embodies my belief that a connection to nature can be transformative. Cultivating the art of nurturing life through sustainable gardening, beginning with the soil, sowing seeds, and participating in the amazing miracle of growth, is a powerful catalyst for positive change. Tending to these gardens allows them to connect with the natural world and will instill a deep sense of responsibility and belonging into their lives.

We believe in providing a safe, supportive, and inclusive space where individuals can explore their inner strength, connect with nature, and tap into their innate power to heal and thrive. Once again, our mission is to change the world, one child, one family, and one person.

This is what World Building looks like.

Chapter 28

Body of Health

Opal M. Venell

I've been married to my wonderful Dave for 38 years and have two awesome children, Daena and Zakery and their spouses, Pablo and Erin, respectively. Plus two sweet granddaughters, Sophia and Lucy. These wonderful humans are so special to me and enrich my life.

I've been a Legal Assistant for 34 years and counting. I work in estate planning, probate, adoptions and corporate law. These experiences are deeply rewarding. I especially love the adoptions because I usually get to see how the children turn out and I hear about their life experiences. I also witness the amazing selflessness of the mothers who put them up for adoption.

I've been a licensed massage therapist for 27 years and counting. I was drawn to this therapy at the age of 18, when I met my sister-in-law. She was studying to become a massage therapist and I fell in love with this fascinating field too.

Who am I??

- ❖ Me
- ❖ Wife
- ❖ Mother
- ❖ Grandmother
- ❖ Friend
- ❖ Legal Assistant
- ❖ Licensed Massage Therapist

When my children were small, I worked full time, went to school and also became a certified and licensed massage therapist. During the weekends I worked on my clients. The therapies I use are: Swedish Massage, Deep Tissue Massage, Healing Touch, Reiki, Cranial Sacral Therapy, Polarity Therapy and Distant Healing.

I incorporate most of these therapies in every session I give. I especially like Cranial Sacral and Polarity Therapy and use them in Distant Healing. Distant Healing is my newest endeavor. I have answered my calling to have been an enthusiastic student and now, an effective practitioner of this for life. This is amazing work and I enjoy and am honored to inspire and improve my clients' lives.

For fun, I love to hike, garden and hang out with my family and my pups, Brewer and Stella. Brewer is a Boxer and has such a personality. As my sister would say, he needs his own show!!! Stella is a Staffordshire Terrier mix and the sweetest thing. She is a hunter but settles down in the evening to snuggle.

I love and appreciate my life!

Balanced, Dynamic and Integrated Massage Therapy, including: Swedish Massage, Deep Tissue Massage, Reiki, Healing Hands, Integrated Cranial Unwinding, Polarity and Distance Healing.

Contact: Opal M. Venell
Phone: 602-448-3353
Website: mybodyofhealth.com
Facebook: Opal Venell, LMT - Body of Health
Email: opalboh@gmail.com

Chapter 29

Thane McWhorter

Thane McWhorter
Grow Healthy-Eat Healthy, LLC Global Aquaponic Project

Grow Healthy-Eat Healthy, LLC
Global Aquaponic Project, GAP, Non-Profit Arm

Since 2007, our founder, Thane McWhorter, has amassed in-depth experience by way of practicing, installing, and designing Aquaponic Systems. This extraordinary urban farming method combines soil-less media and is fertilized by fish. He has a lifetime of cultivating produce and growing food.

In 2007, he received a call from a good friend who asked if he'd ever heard of Aquaponics. I replied, "Yes, that's the process of how tomatoes and medicinal marijuana are grown." His friend informed him that it was hydroponics, not aquaponics, and explained that Aquaponics, in a very short definition, is a "fish-powered garden." It's only been around for about 1500 years! In fact, there are hieroglyphics of the Mayans doing this same growing process. After this fateful introduction, he continued to improve the original concept. This evolution springboarded him to capitalize on his Grandmother Grace's influence and continue his ongoing, current Aquaponics success. It is something he is very passionate about. The deep feeling of "being one with nature" resonates with his entire purpose.

As long as he can remember, he has been gardening. When growing up, he had the pleasure of his grandmother Grace living next door. Their homes were in a central Phoenix's greenbelt area where flood irrigation was a standard process of watering. At 550 gallons per minute for 45 minutes, water came every two weeks for eight months out of the year. His whole property (inside the perimeters created by built-up banks called berms) would flood in some areas over a foot deep. Having these benefits was prime for growing fruits, vegetables, and citrus. He has always had a knack for successfully growing greens. There was something very special about getting his hands in the soil and watching plants manifest before his eyes.

The spring and fall were his favorite times to grow. Everything had so much life; with his family's tender love and care, things grew effortlessly for them. A repository of vegetables replete with nurturing value and different citrus trees such as AZ Sweet Orange, navel orange, pink grapefruit, and Lisbon lemon thrived. They even found a peach tree with four types of peach on one tree whose fruit was harvested at different times, about two months apart.

After his grandmother passed away, he had the opportunity to purchase her home, which he did. His enthusiasm for gardening never stopped; if anything, it grew deeper in the realm of variety. Carnival radishes and carrots, sweet honeydew, cheddar cauliflower, graffiti cauliflower, green stripe tomatoes, etc. If it was out of the ordinary and you did not see it in the store, he was growing it. Baker's Nursery was also a big help because they were the only place that carried those types of heirloom seeds. A wonderful relationship was born with the people at Bakers Nursery. Their friendliness, knowledge, and willingness to always be helpful was greatly appreciated,

In 2014, Thane was hired as the lead developer for the Uganda African non-profit organization Return Hope International. He also worked and consulted with Endless Food Systems and provided plug-and-play aquaponic systems for multiple schools and residential premises. In addition, Thane has an extensive history of 20+ years of hands-on self-employment in construction and sales.

Thane's mission is to bridge the environmental gap of water, wellness, and energy. His ongoing goal is to nurture the human body through pure, clean food and feed the less fortunate one meal at a time. Changing the culture with his astonishing Aquaponics provides the ultra-benefits of a 100% organic urban farming system. By comparison, Aquaponics yields five times the amount of food on the same amount of land required for traditional farming.

Problem:

Today's Agricultural methodology is antiquated! It has a 100% water loss, is ruining our soils with oil-based, synthetic fertilizers, harmful herbicides, and man-made pesticides, and provides unhealthy foods. Global Aquaponic Project (GAP) is based on a thousand-plus year farming system that helps solve hunger and provides nutritionally dense, high-quality food. In addition, GAP's process is a closed, environmental agricultural habitat that realizes only an amazing 5-10% water loss versus traditional farming.

There are billions of people without access to nourishing food. Thane's GAP approach also focuses on educating them about their food and how to feed their families better. As stated, most commercial foods are laced with synthetic fertilizers, oil-based herbicides, and man-made pesticides. Usually, produce is trucked in from an average of 1500 miles away. Aquaponics reduces the carbon footprint. Currently, growing is seasonal due to the changing weather patterns. These limited growing seasons, water shortages, and depleted soils are a worldwide issue.

Solution:

Because of its brilliant recirculation system, growing Aquaponically in a controlled environment uses 90-95% less water than any other agricultural growing method. Growing Aquaponically eliminates the harmful use of oil-based synthetic chemicals. It also requires 87% less energy, drastically cuts fuel costs, and yields year-round food sources. The synthesis process in Aquaponics is scientifically proven to deliver high antioxidant, micro, and macro nutrient-rich foods.

To reach Thane for speaking engagements, residential installations, and any other questions regarding how to create a better future, his email is as follows:

Thane@globalaquaponicproject.org

Visit his website: GlobalAquaponicProject.org.

View our video interview with Thane McWhorter by scanning this QR Code with your smartphone, or go to: https://youtu.be/RWpJN3Nfizk

This modern-day, genuinely magical, mythical, and majestic
Storybook of Fairy Tales, Fables, and Folklore
ignites the imagination of both children and adults.

These sacred storytellers have exquisitely created, crafted,
and cultivated luminous Ava-STARRS,
whose superpowers transport readers to a realm
where the impossible becomes possible.

And the ordinary becomes extraordinary, inspiring them to think
beyond the boundaries of their everyday lives.

Revealed within these daring quests is a treasure trove of
bejeweled stories that unveil courage, enhance life skills,
and bestow unconditional love.

The valuable rewards of perseverance, perspective,
and personal growth, along with perspicacity,
expand, elevate, and enrich the gifts of imagination.
Indeed, we are the stories we tell ourselves.

This is Volume III
of the Guiding Grace Series
You May Also Enjoy...

Volume I
Wisdom of the Silver Sisters

https://amzn.to/4ou4sLj

Volume II
Golden Wisdom of Love, Legends and Legacies

https://amzn.to/3Qz0psp

www.ingramcontent.com/pod-product-compliance
Lightning Source LLC
Chambersburg PA
CBHW051102030726
47504CB00006B/1745